# ROOKIE

## A PODIUM SPORTS ACADEMY BOOK

13-255

# LORNA SCHULTZ
# NICHOLSON

P7-DZO-372

JAMES LORIMER & COMPANY LTD., PUBLISHERS
TORONTO

11.50

James Lorimer & Company Ltd., Publishers acknowledges the support of the Ontario Arts Council. We acknowledge the financial support of the Government of Canada through the Canada Book Fund for our publishing activities. We acknowledge the support of the Canada Council for the Arts which last year invested $24.3 million in writing and publishing throughout Canada. We acknowledge the Government of Ontario through the Ontario Media Development Corporation's Ontario Book Initiative.

**Library and Archives Canada Cataloguing in Publication**

Schultz Nicholson, Lorna
   Rookie / Lorna Schultz Nicholson.

(Podium Sports Academy)
Issued also in electronic formats.
ISBN 978-1-4594-0025-2 (bound).--ISBN 978-1-4594-0024-5 (pbk.)

   I. Title.
   II. Series: Schultz Nicholson, Lorna. Podium Sports Academy.

PS8637.C58R66 2012     jC813'.6     C2012-900034-5

James Lorimer & Company Ltd.,
Publishers
317 Adelaide Street West, Suite 1002
Toronto, ON, Canada
M5V 1P9
www.lorimer.ca

Distributed in the United States by:
Orca Book Publishers
P.O. Box 468
Custer, WA USA
98240-0468

Printed and bound in Canada

Manufactured by Friesens Corporation in Altona, Manitoba, Canada in February 2012. Job #72996

# CHAPTER ONE

"Ice is ready," said Tony Ramsey, standing up. "Rookies go last."

I stayed seated. Tony Ramsey was in his third and final year at Podium Sports Academy High School in Calgary and was the obvious leader of the hockey team. As a graduating student, he was a shoo-in for captain and a bit of a jerk, or so were the rumours.

I snuck a quick glance at my new teammates. Nobody I knew, not one player. Usually I played on a team with friends. In the dressing room before practices, we joked around, laughed, and threw wads of tape, hoping to hit someone in the head before they saw it coming.

I jiggled my leg and breathed deeply to settle my churning stomach. There were only four rookies on the team and I was one of them. And at five foot nine and 160 pounds, I was the smallest.

I didn't move toward the door until everyone had gone, and I mean everyone. Once on the ice, skating in warm-up, my breathing returned to normal. My legs moved naturally underneath me, my blades digging and scraping the freshly cleaned ice, creating a sound I loved. My parents didn't understand my passion for hockey, but I sure did; it was a game of skill, finesse, speed, and grit.

As I skated, I put my stick behind my back, leaned over, and stretched from side to side. My sharpened skates glided along the ice. For years I had dreamed of going to Podium, a school designed for elite athletes of all sports. I knew it would increase my chances to get a college hockey scholarship, have a career in the best sport in the world, and even win a gold medal at the Winter Olympics. I know I dream big. This school was my first step.

I straightened and really started skating, taking the corners with speed as I did my crossovers, then getting low to accelerate on the straightaway. I picked up a loose puck, playing with it on the end of my stick, swishing it along the ice.

A few minutes later, Coach Rennert blew the whistle. I skated to the circle, secured a spot right up front, and got down on one knee. All three coaches were ex-NHL players, and the head coach, Pat Rennert, had coached in the NHL and had decided to take this job so he could help develop young players. Written up in all the top hockey magazines, he was touted to be one of the best.

"You have all been selected for this school and team because of your work ethic, skill, and past performance with your minor hockey organizations," said Coach Rennert. "Some of you have been here before, others are rookies. No matter who you are, you have to work. If you're not working, you'll be benched, and if you still don't work, you'll be sent home."

The excited energy of my teammates gave me shivers. I actually thought I could feel the guys breathing. Not hear them, but feel. Last year I had played on a top Midget team in Vancouver, but it sure didn't have this intensity.

Once Coach Rennert had given the rest of his no-nonsense speech, we were told to head to the end zone for some skating. I raced to be the first one in line. When my coach from last year had heard that I was leaving, he had given me a few hints: make sure I was first out of the dressing room, first on the ice, and first in line to show you were keen.

The skating drills were all ones I'd done before, except the pace was notably quicker. And I considered myself a fast skater. After fifteen minutes of pure skating, no pucks, we were given a water break. Sweat ran down my face when I pushed up my helmet. My heart was still clicking like the metronome my sister had for her music.

"How you doing, *Rookie?*" Tony squirted water into his mouth.

"Good." I wiped my mouth and put my helmet back on. "You're fast."

"Thanks."

"But are you tough?" He smirked at me. For some reason, his scowl made me nervous so I flipped my cage down.

The whistle blew and both of us skated to the circle.

For the next hour we went from drill to drill with no standing around. My feet were kept moving the entire time, and the flow from one drill to the next was as smooth as the fine Chinese silk my mother loved to have shipped from, as she would call it, "the home country."

With fifteen minutes left, Coach Rennert called us in. "We'll do one last drill. If executed properly we'll finish with a few minutes of scrimmage. Battle drill against the boards."

I sucked in a huge gulp of air. This was my least favourite drill because of my size. When my name was called, my heart pounded. I figured out pretty quickly that I was going against one of the biggest guys on the team. The coach threw the puck along the boards and we both charged for it. I got there first, but my opponent was strong on his stick. My arms turned to mush as I pushed him off me in an effort not to be sent flying to the ice. That was the trick of the drill: to get your opponent to cave so you could take the puck and skate away. It was to simulate fighting for the puck along the boards. My heart rate elevated. When was Coach going to call it quits for us?

"Keep going!" yelled Coach Rennert.

I kept pushing and pulling and shoving until I heard him yell, "Time!"

To catch my breath, which was coming in wicked gasps, I had to bend over at the waist. I was still sucking air when I heard Coach say, "Not bad."

When practice ended, I flopped down on the bench in the dressing room like a beached fish, leaned against the wall, and closed my eyes. That had been the toughest practice of my entire life.

"Where you from?" the guy beside me asked.

I opened my eyes and looked at him. "Vancouver. You?"

"Toronto."

"This your first year?"

"Yeah."

"Me too." I held out my sweaty palm. "Aaron Wong."

He shook my hand and smiled. "Kade Jensen."

I had only just taken off my skates, shoulder pads, and elbows pads when Tony got to his feet. "Listen up!"

When he had everyone's attention, he said, "Rookie party on Saturday night. My house. And this is just our team. Do not breathe a word of this to anyone. Not even the coaches."

"Right on," said Steven Kilby. He sat on my other side and was good friends with Ramsey. He was also graduating this year. "Nothing like an old-fashioned rookie party."

I turned to Kade and whispered, "Rookie party?"

He shrugged. "It's a party."

My stomach knotted. Being a logical thinker, I didn't have the same confidence that this party was just a party. Wasn't it just last year that a rookie party had gone downhill fast at some U.S. school and a guy had died of alcohol poisoning?

# CHAPTER TWO

The next morning my alarm went off at 5:45. I groaned. The early mornings were definitely something I would have to get used to. Two days a week we had yoga before school, because it was supposed to help our core strength. The other three days we did weights and dryland.

I got dressed in under five minutes, slung my backpack over my shoulder, then tiptoed up the stairs. At this time of the morning, my entire billet family was still asleep and the house was dark, quiet, and unbelievably weird. I was still getting used to living in a billet house, with a family other than my own, and foraging for food in a strange refrigerator. They had told me to make myself at home, but it was harder than I thought.

My bedroom was in the basement and my billet family had bedrooms upstairs. The arrangement worked for me. I liked my privacy. They had two kids: eight-year-old Jordan and six-year-old Samantha. Jordan liked me and was constantly in my room bugging me, but I didn't have a little brother, so I didn't mind. Mr. and Mrs. Dylan seemed really nice, especially when they welcomed me and met my parents. At least my mom had been civil. When we were out of the Dylans' earshot, though, she had gone on about how I wouldn't get enough real Chinese food to eat. I told her I'd go to the mall on the weekends and grab some from the vendors, and did she know that Ginger Beef was actually invented in Calgary? That bit of trivia made her go ballistic. That was not *real* Chinese.

The fridge light illuminated the room. I took out a chunk of cheese and an apple, then shut the door. A paper-bagged lunch sat on the kitchen counter with my name on it, and I stuffed it into my backpack. Then I went outside to wait for the little school bus that picked students up every morning. There were separate buses for every sport.

The air was crisp and a whole lot colder than the coldest winter day on the West Coast. And it was only September. There was even frost on the ground already. I shivered and pulled my hoodie over my head. That was another thing my mother worried about: how I, a Vancouver kid, was going to survive a winter in Calgary.

When the letter came last spring inviting me to attend Podium, I couldn't believe it. That night at dinner, I showed my parents the letter and my mother started speaking Chinese at a rate that even my grandmother wouldn't have understood, her shrill high voice pinging off the walls. It took me days to convince my parents that it was a good school because: (1) I was on a scholarship so they didn't have to pay anything and (2) I could potentially get a scholarship for a U.S. college.

The bus picked me up and I sat in the first available seat. It was way too early for anyone to talk. Then the yoga room was hot and I almost fell asleep, though I have to admit the stretching was challenging. Kade was beside me on a mat, but we didn't talk, because the instructor told us you're not supposed to talk in a yoga class.

When at last the bus dropped us off at school, Kade waited for me. "What do you have first?" he asked as we walked toward the front door of the school.

"Physics," I answered. "What about you?"

"Math. Which I suck at."

I shrugged. Math was fairly easy for me. English was my nemesis.

"Are you taking grade eleven or twelve?" I asked.

My parents' allowing me to come to the school came with stipulations. I had to keep every mark above ninety-five or they would yank me. That meant English too. Academics ruled in my house. I was lucky I had inherited my dad's talent for math.

"Eleven," Kade replied, sounding surprised. "What are you in?"

"I fast-tracked last year so I'm taking twelve. Opens my options. Next year I can take calculus."

He punched my arm and grinned. "Are you some sort of brain? Can you tutor me?"

"Yeah, probably."

"I need all the help I can get."

He held his hand up and we smacked a high-five. It sure felt good to have a friend.

"What was your old school like?" he asked.

"Huge." I laughed. "At least four thousand kids."

"Yeah, mine too in Toronto. This is so weird going to a

school with just two hundred kids."

Podium Sports Academy was a fairly new building on the outskirts of Calgary. When the decision to create such a school was made five years ago, sponsors were found for the funding. The place was amazing. It had regular classrooms, but a fantastic workout facility, plus a double gymnasium. We'd had an orientation yesterday but no classes yet, so I hadn't met anyone from the other sports.

"Hey Kade," I said. I paused, trying to think how to say what I wanted to say without sounding like a loser. "This rookie party on Saturday night, do you know much about it?" Last night I woke up with the sweats, because I'd had a terrible dream about the party.

"Not really. I know Tony Ramsey lives at home. He doesn't billet. I think his mom moved here this year, for his grad year. His parents are divorced."

"Did they have a rookie party last year?" I tried to sound nonchalant.

"Not sure. Hey, we should crash the Sir Winston dance on Friday night. Could be fun. They say Sir Winston Churchill is the biggest high school in the city." He raised his eyebrows. "Girls."

"Sure," I replied. Having no social life was my biggest concern coming to this school. This would give me something to do on my first Friday night in Calgary.

"If you're up for it, I'll try to score some beer or something." Kade looked at me out of the corner of his eye, obviously wondering if he had crossed a line.

"Okay," I said. We'd had a lecture yesterday about drinking — if a student was caught drinking, he or she would be expelled. But I didn't want to look lame in front of my first friend.

We entered the front lobby of the school. "You want to meet for lunch?" Kade asked.

"I'm going to have to buy," I said. "I ate my entire lunch on the bus."

"So did I," Kade laughed. "My billets didn't give me near enough. There's a Subway at a little strip mall down the road."

"Meet you here and we can walk over," I said. After confirming our lunch plans, Kade and I went in different directions.

I entered my physics class and sat down at the first empty desk I saw. I glanced around and couldn't help wondering which sport each kid was in. I didn't see any of my hockey teammates. When a tall, and I mean really tall, African-Canadian girl with long straightened black hair walked in and sat beside me, I decided her sport was either volleyball or basketball. She had to be six-one, with legs that would probably come up to my armpits. She plunked a book on the desk in front of her, saving a seat for someone, probably another tall girl I wouldn't have a hope with. On my other side, a guy was slouched at his desk. He wore a toque, so I thought he might be a snowboarder. I knew I was stereotyping, but he did look the part. Then it dawned on me that they might be evaluating me, as well. I wondered if I looked like a hockey player.

Just as the teacher arrived, a shorter girl walked in, with her blond ponytail bouncing, and other things bouncing too. I knew I was staring but I couldn't help it. She was hot.

"Hey, Carrie," whispered the tall girl. "I saved you a seat."

Carrie slipped into the seat in front of the tall girl, so was kitty-corner to me and within my peripheral vision. She turned around and whispered, "Thanks, Allie." Then she made a face. "I so hate physics." She had a perfect nose and mouth. *Stop staring*, said my brain. But my body didn't listen.

The teacher started to talk and Carrie turned around to face the front. For the first few minutes I missed what the teacher was saying because I was trying to figure out Carrie's sport. She wasn't total muscle like the compact gymnasts, or skinny like the synchro swimmers, or tall like the volleyball and basketball players. Perhaps she was a volleyball setter with a great vertical. Or she could be a snowboarder, but she didn't dress the part. They usually wore baggy clothes like cargo pants . . . and she was *not* wearing baggy clothing. Everything clung to her body as if it had been painted on, just the way I liked it on girls. Okay, maybe she was a skier . . . ?

Luckily my mind shifted to what the teacher was saying, because if I didn't stop thinking about Carrie, I'd fail physics. And that wouldn't sit well with my parents. Within minutes I was back up to speed with the physics principles, and I totally understood the equations. When the teacher handed out the homework at the end of class, I figured it would take me all of twenty minutes to complete.

On the way out, I walked behind Carrie, staring at her back and, well, other things. How could I not? I liked girls who weren't super skinny, who had some meat on their bones. And she had that, in all the right places.

"Why did he have to give us so much homework?" I heard Carrie complain to Allie. "I have a three-hour practice tonight. We're working on this insane routine."

Routine? She can't be a skier, I thought. Unless she was into freestyle. I shook my head. My thoughts were cruising through my brain way too fast.

"I can try to help," said Allie. "Although I don't think I get it much more than you do. Hey, you want to go to the Sir Winston dance on Friday night?"

Carrie nodded. "Yeah, okay."

It was at times like this that I wished I was *that* guy. You know, the one who can just swagger up to a girl and start talking. If I was, I could have just stepped in, offered to help with their homework, and then told them I was going to the dance too. But no, I lowered my head and kept enough distance between us so that I wouldn't bump into them if they suddenly stopped.

At the hall intersection, they went the opposite way from where I was going. I would just have to wait until physics class to see Carrie again. I checked the schedule taped to my binder and was jacked to see I had physics again tomorrow.

# CHAPTER THREE

I met Kade in the front lobby at lunchtime and we walked over to Subway. The weather was so weird in Calgary. Early in the morning it had been freezing, and now, partway through the day, it was as hot as a summer day in Vancouver. I had to take off my hoodie and wrap it around my waist.

"Math is so hard already," Kade moaned.

"It's only the first day."

"I know." Then he grinned. "But I met a super-hot volleyball player."

"That was fast."

"She was in my math class and hates it as much as I do."

"They're all tall."

"That's cool with me."

"Because you're six-three. I'm only five-nine."

"Sucks to be you." Kade laughed. "You'll just have to hook up with the gymnasts or skiers."

"There was a girl in my physics class and she might be a skier. Her name's Carrie."

"Carrie. I know a Carrie who's at this school. If it's the

same Carrie, we come from the same city and she's into synchro. Blond, about this tall." He held up his hand to show me the height and he was right on.

"This one didn't look like a synchro swimmer. I mean, she was . . ."

Kade burst out laughing. "She's got 'em, all right. Back home they called her Curvy Carrie. I bet it's the same girl." Then he broke into a run. "Come on. I'm starving. Buy me lunch and I'll introduce you to her later."

I had a twenty-dollar bill out of my pocket before we arrived at Subway.

I didn't see Carrie or Kade again that afternoon, so the introduction was going to have to wait. At the end of classes, I was on a bus heading to hockey practice. Time to shift my focus.

One of the other rookies, Ben Hamilton, sat across from Kade and me on the bus. I had a feeling the rookies stuck together and weren't really included until they had proven themselves on the ice. Everyone was talking about the tournament we were going to the following weekend at Shattuck–St. Mary's School in Faribault, Minnesota.

I wondered how much ice time I would get. I had been warned that rookies didn't get that much their first year at this school. Being in grade eleven already, I had to somehow get noticed by the scouts, at least show up on their radar, and that meant I had to play.

My former coach told me that no matter how many shifts I played, every one had to be good, and if I only got one a period, it had to be phenomenal. Last year I was on the power play and the penalty kill, and played just about every other shift in tight games. I logged big minutes.

I didn't want to be the rookie sitting on the bench. With that thought planted firmly in my mind, I worked my butt off in practice: skating, shooting, checking, and working hard along the boards, like yesterday. I made sure I didn't back down from anyone. At the camp I attended in the summer, all the comments were the same: good skater, good stick handling, but needs to work on toughness, two-way play, and defensive skills. I had taken boxing lessons in the summer to help me become a tougher player.

"Yesterday we didn't get to scrimmage," said Coach Rennert at the end of practice. "We have five minutes left. Split up and make the teams even."

Somehow Kade, Ben, and I ended up on the same team and the same line: three rookies. Sure didn't look like the teams were even. The other rookie, a six-foot-four defenceman named Kurt Jones, managed to get on the other team with Tony and Steven and another good player, Max Morris.

"We could get creamed," said Kade as we waited on the bench for our turn to play.

I looked at Ben and Kade. "If we get out against the good line, we have to show them up."

"Yeah," they both said.

When it was our turn, we played against Tony, Max, and Steven. They had Kurt on defence, and it was obvious why. If Coach Rennert tried to accuse them of stacking their line, they could claim they had a rookie.

"Let's do it," I said. I jumped on the ice and kicked into

high gear right away. Last summer I worked on my first three strides so I could have explosive power. I'd gone to a trainer in Kelowna who had an indoor stride machine.

I got to the puck first. I picked it up without breaking stride, and at full speed skated toward the goalie. Kade moved with me. Out of the corner of my eye, I saw Tony coming. I accelerated, skated to the outside, and once I was over the blue line, I drop-passed the puck to Kade. Then I felt the stick around my body, the hook. I used all my strength and pushed Tony away, then bolted for the net. Kade gave me the pass and I rifled top shelf. The puck was sitting in the back of the net when I felt the crush of a stick against my back. Fortunately, when I fell, I missed the posts.

I got up and brushed the snow off my pants.

"Nice goal," said Kade.

"Great pass," I replied.

Lined up on the bench, Ben turned to me and said, "Ramsey's got your number."

"Doubt it."

"You beat him one on one, dude. He's dirty when he's pissed. And he's known to pick on anyone who threatens his position."

I shrugged. "That's okay by me. It'll make me tougher. I'm no good to this team if I don't work to get on the first line."

When practice ended, I tossed my equipment into my bag and thought about dinner. I hoped my billets had made something like spaghetti. I could use some carbs.

"Team meeting tomorrow at lunch," yelled Tony.

"Except rookies." Max threw a wad of tape at Kurt. Kurt picked it up and threw it back. Max nodded at Kurt. "You're okay."

Then Steven Kilby threw a wad of tape at me. I figured I should do the same as Kurt, so I leaned over to pick it up. I was about to throw it back when I heard Tony say, "Don't even think about it, Wong. You're a rookie."

For some reason, I tossed the tape on the floor. Afterward, I wondered if I'd done the right thing. Was Tony testing me? I had beaten him on the ice but had just let him beat me *off* the ice. He looked at me and snickered. Then he stood and put his towel around his waist. "Rookies go last in the shower. And, Wong, you are dead last. Dead. Last."

"Told you," whispered Ben. "Watch your back. Ramsey plays dirty on and off the ice."

# CHAPTER FOUR

That night we did have spaghetti for dinner, plus meatballs and salad, and I piled my plate high. Jordan laughed. "I bet you can't eat all that."

I smiled at him from across the dinner table as I tore my bun in two. I still found it strange to be eating dinner with a family other than my own. No one spoke Chinese. Although, to be honest, at home we hardly ever ate dinner together because my younger sister, Erica, played the trumpet and piano and was always at some kind of lesson, and I played Triple-A hockey, so I was out almost every night. Her playing the trumpet was like me playing hockey. My parents weren't thrilled. But they liked her playing the piano.

"Bet you I can," I said.

"How much should we bet?" Jordan bopped up and down in his seat.

Mrs. Dylan smiled at Jordan. "You don't have any money to bet, young man."

"Why do you always have to wreck things?" He slumped in his chair.

"Okay, no betting, but if I eat all this, I'll play mini-sticks with you," I said, winking at him.

"You'll play with me after dinner? Cool! I wanna be goalie."

"Do you have much homework, Aaron?" Mrs. Dylan asked, smiling at me.

"Not too much." I tried to speak between mouthfuls of food so I wouldn't look rude. My mother had drilled some manners into me before I left.

"That's good," said Mrs. Dylan.

*Good?* I had to stifle a laugh. At home if I didn't say I had at least two hours, my parents would think the teachers weren't doing their jobs. All last year, I'd lied and told them I had tons, then went to my room and either played video games or messed around on Facebook. I couldn't help it that math came easy to me.

"How are your practices going?" Mr. Dylan asked.

"Great."

"I've heard Rennert runs a good practice."

"Yeah. They're the best I've ever had."

He glanced at his son. "Jordan and I are pretty excited to go to your first home game."

"What about me?" squeaked Samantha. "I wanna go too."

"And me," said Mrs. Dylan.

"It's a family affair, then!" declared Jordan. Everyone at the table laughed at his joke and I felt good. These people wanted to watch me play hockey. My parents hardly ever came to watch.

I helped clear the dishes and load the dishwasher before Jordan and I played mini-sticks. He grumbled the entire time he waited, wondering when I was going to be done.

I let him play net. Some shots I let him make the save on purpose. We'd been playing for around twenty minutes when my cell phone rang.

"I gotta get this." I put my stick down.

"Why?" he whined. "I was making such good saves."

I looked at the number displayed on the screen and didn't recognize it. "Practice without me for a sec," I said before saying hello.

"Is this Aaron?" The voice was a girl's.

"Yeah."

"Um, are you in Mr. Keene's physics class? First period?"

"Yeah. Who is this?"

"Oh, sorry, my name is Carrie and I'm a friend of Kade's. I think you and me are in the same class."

My throat closed and I wasn't sure I was going to be able to talk. Saliva sat on my tongue like a huge wad of gum. "Oh," was all I could muster.

"Come on, play mini-sticks." Jordan tugged at my jeans. I held up my finger to tell him one minute, then moved to the corner of the room for privacy.

"Have you done your physics homework yet?" Carrie asked. "Kade told me to call you. I can't do the third question."

"I'll get my books," I said. Then I put my hand over the phone and said to Jordan, "I have to do homework."

His bottom lip jutted out.

"We'll play tomorrow." I patted him on the head, then raced down the stairs to my bedroom and my books. I had to get them open and to question three fast.

"I'm so sorry," she said. "Did I catch you at a bad moment?"

"No, it's okay," I said. "I just have a little boy at my billets' who likes me to play mini-sticks."

"Oh, that's so cute. I billet with a couple whose kids have grown and moved out. They like the company, even though I'm not around a ton."

"What sport are you in?" Of course, I already knew the answer, but I had to make conversation.

"Synchro. Now about question three. I have to get this done. I'm in the pool by six tomorrow morning."

The question wasn't hard and I walked her through the equation to get the answer. When we were done, she said, "Thank you *so* much."

"Any time," I replied. And like an idiot, that's all I said. I wanted to mention the dance on Friday night, but my tongue swelled in my mouth.

"I'll introduce myself tomorrow in class," she said.

I didn't want to tell her I already knew who she was, so I said, "Sure."

"Where were you sitting today?"

"Um, kind of in the middle. Beside a really tall girl."

"You were beside Allie?" She sounded confused.

My heart sank to my toes. I hadn't even made an impression. "Yeah. Is that her name?" I managed.

The phone went silent. I closed my eyes. Damn. Obviously she was trying to recall who'd been sitting beside Allie.

After a couple of seconds, I decided to make it easier for her. "I'm the only Chinese kid in the class. My last name is Wong."

She started to laugh. "O-kay, I remember you now. Well, see you tomorrow, Aaron *Wong*. And thanks again. I really appreciate your help."

I hung up the phone and immediately fell to one knee and did the classic hockey victory pump. I would definitely get to talk to her tomorrow.

# CHAPTER FIVE

I gritted my teeth. *I can do this. I can do this.* I ran the mantra through my head. I blew out a huge rush of air as I did the bench press. The weight was more than I'd ever pressed before.

Kade stood behind me, ready to catch it if I struggled.

I closed my eyes and pressed again. It was incredibly heavy, but I kept going.

"You got it," encouraged Kade.

My cheeks bulged.

"Breathe," said Kade. "And push."

I exhaled and thrust the weight up. I held it for a split second once it was up there, then I racked it. Blood pumped through my body. Stars swirled in front of my face. I had done it. I sat up.

"Good job." Kade held up his hand and I weakly smacked it.

"Thanks, Jensen."

I glanced around the room at my teammates. We had been split into pairs and I was glad to have been put with Kade. Ramsey and Kilby were together, but that was to be expected, and Max was with Kurt, who seemed to have worked his way into the upper echelon a lot quicker than the other rookies. Size spoke.

I was starting to learn a few nicknames. Ramsey was Rammer and Kilby was Killer. Ben was paired with the funny guy on the team, Mitchell Mayer, and they called him Hot Dog because he liked hot dogs and his last name went with Oscar Mayer Wieners. The rumour was he could eat five in one sitting. Ben's nickname was Hammy and had been for years. It was a no-brainer. I had always been Wonger, but as of yet, the only guys who called me that were Kade and Ben.

The rest called me Wong.

"How much you lift, Wong?" Ramsey yelled from across the room.

"One-eighty."

"Bull."

"He did," said Kade.

"Shut up, Jensen. I wasn't talking to you. Wong, why do you lie?"

"Whatever." I shook my head.

Kade rolled his eyes. "Let's just finish our workout."

Afterward, tired and sore, I hit the shower. As the warm water drenched my skin, I wondered if Ramsey really was out to get me. I shut the water off and grabbed my towel off the rack. As I walked out of the shower area with my head down, someone punched my shoulder. Hard. It knocked me off balance and I fell to the floor.

Ramsey and Kilby laughed.

"What was that for, Rammer?" I asked. How could

this guy be our captain?

"Don't call me Rammer. That's for friends only."

For the second time that morning, I said, "Whatever." I had no desire to get in a fight with any of my teammates. Last I heard, hockey was a team sport.

I pulled my carefully folded jeans out of my bag and breathed a sigh of relief. They weren't crumpled. Last night I had laid my clothes out on the bed before packing my bag. It had taken me some time to get the right jeans and the right shirt. I had opted for a button-down shirt instead of a T-shirt; I wanted to look like a well-dressed hockey player.

I dressed quickly and went to the mirror to fix my hair. Then I heard the bellow "Bus is here!"

"Did Carrie phone you last night?" Kade grinned as we walked to the bus.

"Yeah."

"You owe me."

"I bought you a sub."

"I heard she's going to the dance Friday."

"Hook me up and I'll buy you a foot-long." I punched his arm.

"A hookup is good for at least two. And getting you booze is another one, so you owe me three."

"Sounds decent." Although I had just had my first beer this past summer at a BBQ, I figured I would need *some* alcohol if I was going to talk to her.

I sucked in a big breath just before I entered the physics class. When I walked in, I tried to look cool. Carrie was already sitting in the same desk as yesterday. My seat was also open, so I slid in and . . . just sat there, stupidly, like a geek. So much for being cool. With her books already opened, Carrie looked focused on her physics, not me. I swallowed. I breathed. In and out. And I rubbed my hands on my thighs. All I had to do was reach over and touch her on the shoulder and say hi. *I can do this. I can do this.* The talk in my head had worked this morning in dryland, but it sure wasn't working now.

I had one hand lifted to tap her on the shoulder when Allie flopped down in the seat beside me with a groan. Carrie immediately turned around. "Hey, what's up? I know that sound."

Allie slouched in her desk, extending her long legs. "I'm screwed. I didn't get my math done or my physics."

Carrie did a little dance with her hands as she sang, "I got my physics done. I got my physics done." She looked over at me and grinned. "Hey, Aaron, when did you get here? Thanks again."

"Uh, I just got here." I tapped my pencil on the desk, then stopped when I realized how elementary school it was to tap-tap your pencil.

"Allie," said Carrie, "Aaron can help you with physics. He's a genius."

"I'm not a genius," I said, hoping no one else in the class heard her say that.

"Oh my gawd, could you?" Allie reached over and placed her hand on my arm. "Please, please, please. I had practice last night and it went late. I was so tired when I got home and I tried to do it, but I just didn't get it." She let go of my arm and playfully smacked Carrie on the back. "And I called you, girl, and you had gone to bed already."

"I had to be up at five. I don't get to sleep in like you basketball players."

"Hey, I get up early three times a week." Allie stuck her tongue out at Carrie. Then she turned back to me. "So when can we get together?"

Carrie clapped her hands, smiled, and said, "How about lunch? We could all meet and I could get some help with today's homework. Wink, wink."

"Works for me," I said. "As long as one of you has food. I ate my lunch already and was going to Subway."

"You can have mine," said Carrie. "My billets pack me way too many carbs."

When I told Kade my lunch plans, he high-fived me. "Way to go, man."

"Join us," I said.

"Cool. I got a bigger lunch today."

Over lunch I did my best to explain the physics homework, but it seemed we laughed more than mastered equations. Carrie gave me her lunch, which was a massive ham, cheese, lettuce, and pickle sandwich. And her Oreo cookies. She ate the carrot sticks, cucumber slices, and apple. Kade had a double lunch because he had talked to his billets about his need for more food.

The conversation veered to the weekend. "I've got a free day Sunday," said Carrie, leaning back in her seat. "I can hardly believe it. I'm going to sleep in till noon."

"We have Sunday off too," said Kade.

"We might need it after Saturday night," I replied.

"Why? What's on Saturday night?" Carrie asked.

"Nothing," I said quickly.

Allie eyed me. Then she said, "You guys are having one of those stupid rookie parties. "They are gross. You'll probably have to eat and drink weird things." Then her face turned all serious. "Hope those idiots don't try anything dangerous."

The horrible feeling I'd felt last night returned, making my throat dry up instantly. Why would she say that? Did they do something last year?

"I used to love that show *Fear Factor*." Kade grinned, clearly not fazed by Allie's comment. "I can handle eating weird stuff. I could have won the million dollars hands down. But let's get down to real business if we're talking eating and *drinking* stuff." He turned to me and asked, "We still on for the dance, dude?"

"Yeah." I glanced at Carrie, hoping she'd say they were going to the dance too. When she smiled at me, her perfect white teeth glistened under the fluorescent lighting, and I shivered. Then the cold in my body suddenly disappeared and my cheeks started to scorch with heat. I looked down in embarrassment.

"Hey, we're going to that too," she said. "Right, Allie?"

I breathed. *Yes. She mentioned the dance.*

"Sweet," said Kade. "Let's pre-drink together."

"Dunno 'bout that," replied Allie, slouching in her seat, crossing her arms, and shaking her head. "Remember the lecture on no drinking. What if we get caught? My parents would kill me if I got kicked out of this school."

The heat in my cheeks was now gone, so I looked up to get in on the conversation. "We won't get caught," said Kade. "No one has to know but us."

"Yeah, it's not like we're going to know a ton of people at the dance," said Carrie.

"Oh shoot!" Allie jumped up. "We better get to class." She picked up her books.

"So we on for Friday, Dollface?" Carrie scrunched up her nose. "It'll be fun."

"I'll go but I'm the DD," Allie said. "I don't drink, re-member. And you don't either, Carrie. Think about what happened last time."

I glanced at Carrie. What had happened last time?

When we walked out of the cafeteria, I made sure I was walking with Carrie. She was really quiet and seemed deep in thought, and I wondered if she'd prefer I got lost. It took me half a hallway before I said, "If you like, I could help you with your homework on Sunday."

"Are you kidding? That would be great!" She turned and flashed those perfect white teeth again. Relief washed over me; her quietness had nothing to do with me.

If I hadn't been in a school hallway, and in a new school, with a girl I'd just met, I would've kissed her on the spot. Okay, that's a lie. I wouldn't have. We just met. And I was kind of inexperienced with girls. But boy, did I want to. *Maybe Friday night?*

# CHAPTER SIX

Friday dragged. I couldn't wait until the evening and the dance. Actually I was more anxious about the before-dance activities.

As I headed out that night, Mrs. Dylan said, "Who are you going to the dance with?"

"Just a few kids from school."

"Do you have a ride home?"

I nodded and smiled. "Yeah, I should be okay."

Then she smiled back and it made me feel a little guilty. Kade and I were going over to Carrie's to drink before — her billets would be out. All the billets had got the same list of rules, so I knew Mrs. Dylan knew I wasn't supposed to drink. "I'll leave the light on," she said. "Jordan has an early practice tomorrow."

"Thanks. I'll be quiet."

I caught the C-Train on Calgary's transportation system, and halfway there, Kade jumped on to join me. He wore a backpack that looked heavy.

As soon as he sat down beside me, he patted his backpack and whispered, "Tequila, dude. We're going for it. My brother has a friend who goes to the University of Calgary and he booted for me." Then speaking in a normal tone, he said, "Are you going to try to hook up with Carrie tonight?"

I shrugged. "I dunno. Maybe."

We got off the C-Train and walked to Carrie's. She opened the door for us before we even knocked.

"I've been waiting. My billets left fifteen minutes ago. I've even got the limes cut." She seemed nervous. "Kade told me he was bringing tequila — my drink of choice."

We were in the kitchen and on our second tequila shot when Allie showed up. I couldn't believe Carrie. She was actually keeping up to us. Well, I guess two shots weren't *that* many. Maybe she was as nervous as I was.

"Hi, Allie! Come on in." Carrie's voice was loud and high. I laughed when she stood and knocked over the bowl of limes. "Whoops." She put her hand to her mouth and giggled.

"How many have you had, Carrie?" Allie walked into the kitchen, waving her hands. "What are you doing? You're not a drinker. You guys are asking for trouble. What if someone finds out and tells the school?"

"Relax, Allie," said Kade.

Carrie giggled again and did a little dance. "Yeah, relax, Allie. No one will find out. What's that song?" She started to sing. "'Re-lax don't do it. Baby, baby, don't do it.'"

"You've had enough," said Allie, grabbing the tequila bottle off the table.

"Yeah, probably." Carrie's words were a bit slurred. "But Kade is an old friend from home so I thought this would be fun and . . . safe."

"I bet you didn't eat anything to absorb the alcohol."

"You sound like a textbook." Carrie's bottom lip jutted out. "I'm just having fun for once." Then, unexpectedly, she plunked herself down on my lap. Shocked, but pleasantly so, I didn't object.

Allie looked at me and Kade. "No more for her."

"C'mon, one more for the road," said Kade. He held out his hand to Allie. "Bottle, please."

She pursed her lips, then huffed, "All right, but this is it."

"Me too, me too," said Carrie, clapping her hands.

Kade poured three more shots. I shook some salt on my hand, then passed the shaker to Carrie. She grinned at me.

"Let's hook arms."

"You're on." Her skin against mine felt awesome. When I slid my arm under hers, we automatically moved into each other. I could feel her breasts against my arm and thought I might go crazy. Man, they were big and soft and firm all at the same time.

"Ready," said Kade.

We all lifted our glasses, then downed the shots. The tequila burned my throat and made my eyes water, and I could feel it hit the bottom of my stomach. I shook my head and licked the salt off my hand. With her face scrunched up in the classic tequila pucker, Carrie quickly dropped my arm and reached for a lime.

"Okay, that's enough," said Allie. "I don't want you guys puking in my car. Let's clean up and get going."

We all piled into Allie's car, Kade in front, and Carrie and me in the back seat.

"This is only the second time I've been drunk," she

said. "Will you dance with me?"

"I guess so." I wasn't much of a dancer but . . . what the heck.

Kade turned around, laughing. "Hockey players are the worst dancers in the world."

"Shut up." I swatted the back of his head and he reached over the seat to swat me back.

"Stop it," said Allie. "All you hockey boys do is scrap. Not in my car, y'hear?"

When we arrived at Sir Winston Churchill High, Allie found a parking spot in the farthest corner of the lot. "Hopefully a walk will sober you guys up," she said. Then she handed us all some gum. "If they even smell alcohol, we get kicked out."

"We have to act sober," Carrie whispered in my ear. Then she held up her finger. "Shhh. Don't talk. Just walk." Her eyelids drooped.

"Aaron!" commanded Allie. "Hold on to her and act normal."

I wasn't that drunk, so I put my arm around Carrie. She leaned her head against my chest. "You feel good," she said. "Remember, you promised you'd dance."

"Oh my gawd," said Allie. "Girl, you make me crazy."

"I'm okay," said Carrie. "Aaron's a nice guy. Not like —"

"Yeah, okay," Allie interrupted. "Just don't say a freaking word till we're through the gym doors. All of you."

"Okay, boss lady." Kade saluted Allie.

"Shut up," she said.

We made it past the teachers and through the gym doors, mainly because Allie was on top of our arrival.

The gym was dimly lit and packed, groups of kids milling about. Music blared through speakers. Carrie moved away slightly and started shimmying and shaking and . . . I couldn't stop looking at her.

"I loooove this song," said Carrie. "Come on. All four of us."

With Carrie pulling my arm, we headed to the dance floor. I gave it my best effort to move in time with the music. After a few seconds, Kade burst out laughing. "Dude, you are pathetic."

Laughing along with him, I tried to get him in a headlock, but he squirmed out of it. We wrestled for a few seconds, pushing and shoving and just being stupid while the girls continued to dance. I finally had him in a decent headlock when I heard a familiar voice.

"Good hold, Wong."

I looked up. Tony Ramsey stood just outside our little circle.

"Hey Tony." I dropped my arms and for some dumb reason stood ramrod still. Kade glanced at me and I glanced at Kade. Obviously Ramsey had the same effect on Kade. Why? I wasn't totally sure except that he was a veteran and we were rookies. If he caught us drinking and it got back to Coach, we'd be in big trouble. I just hoped Carrie would keep quiet.

"Who you here with?" Kade asked lightly. I thought he sounded normal.

"Couple of friends. Churchill has the best dances." Then he looked at Carrie and smiled, raising his eyebrows at the same time. "Remember last year?"

Carrie stepped forward and inwardly I groaned. She poked Ramsey's chest with her finger. "Go away." Her words were slightly slurred.

He grabbed her hand and yanked her close. "You been drinking?"

"No," she said, pulling away.

"You're fun when you're drunk."

"You're such a jerk." She looked as if she was going to cry. Did Carrie have a thing with Ramsey? I watched him watching her.

Suddenly Carrie stomped on his toes, breaking the moment and causing Ramsey to yelp and jump up and down, grabbing his foot. He was wearing flip-flops and she wore heels. She ducked behind me.

For some reason — perhaps nervousness combined with tequila, or the fact that Carrie had looked at Ramsey like they had something once — I started to laugh. "Dude, you got rocked!"

Surprisingly Ramsey laughed along with me. "Ain't that the truth. She can rock me any time."

Then he gave me a buddy-to-buddy slap on the back and held up his fist for Kade to punch. "I hope you guys are in this kind of mood tomorrow night."

"I'll be ready," said Kade.

"Good team spirit, Jensen. What about you, Wong? You on for the *team event*?"

"Yeah," I said. "Should be good."

Ramsey gave us a finger wave and said, "Till tomorrow."

# CHAPTER SEVEN

Saturday morning I woke up with a feeling of dread in my stomach. I couldn't figure it out. Ramsey had been okay last night. I had nothing to fear about the rookie party. Maybe the dread had more to do with what I had seen happen between Carrie and Ramsey. I knew I couldn't compete with him in the girl department.

What had gone on between them? I wanted to ask Carrie last night, but that would have gone over like a sack of bricks. Carrie was super quiet the entire ride home and I was pretty sure she'd been crying in the bathroom with Allie. So if I had asked her, Allie would have smacked me for sure. And I didn't get to ask Kade either. Allie had dropped us off at our billets so we didn't have to catch the train.

I flung my covers off and got up. No sense lying in bed all day. We didn't have practice or dryland today, so I decided to go for a run.

I liked running. It always did a lot to clear my mind. After about fifty minutes, I was sweating like crazy and winding my way back through the neighbourhood streets, thinking that I was getting worked up about nothing.

I spent the rest of the day doing homework, so I could help Carrie the next day, and watching the stash of *Entourage* DVDs I'd brought from home.

Kade and I had agreed to go to the party together. I got dressed and met Kade in the C-Train again.

"I'll be so glad to get this over with," I said.

He play-punched my arm. "It'll be okay," he said.

*Okay*. What exactly did that mean? *Okay* was a word that could mean a whole lot of things. I was surprised Kade seemed kind of nervous too.

Tony Ramsey's house was located near the University of Calgary, so it was a short walk from the C-Train stop to his address. Kade and I didn't talk much, just walked with our hands in our pockets.

Ramsey greeted us at the door, beer bottle in hand, and slapped our backs. "All right. Here are the last two rookies now!" He didn't look me in the eye and I took that as a good sign: no scowl, no narrowed eyes, no sadistic grin. Maybe he was a different guy outside the changing room. He took a swig of his beer and ushered us inside.

Loud noise filtered from the kitchen to the front hallway and I guessed that just about the entire team had arrived already. When I entered the kitchen, someone sprayed whipped cream on my face. Laughing, I tried to lick it off. If this was what was going to happen, this could be a fun party. I didn't see his mother anywhere, but I sure saw a lot of empty beer and liquor bottles. How long had they been drinking?

Kade laughed too. Suddenly someone wrapped a blind-fold over my eyes. I had no idea who it was until I heard the voice.

"We got your slanty eyes covered," Ramsey hissed in my ear.

Something about his tone of voice alerted something in my body. I shivered. And it had nothing to do with the stupid comment. *Slanty eyes.* I was so tired of this shit. I'd heard comments all my life about being Chinese. Then Kade was laughing again and I shook off the bad feelings. My mind was racing and I had to slow it down. *Relax. Relax. Breathe. Don't panic.*

"Who has the razors?" yelled Ramsey.

"I do," replied Killer.

"Let's do Jensen first."

Someone pushed me into a chair. "Don't move." I recognized Max's voice.

I heard a lot of scuffling and yelling, and I had no idea what was happening until I heard Kade laughing. "Stop! That tickles!" he said. I could tell he was rolling around the floor.

"Someone hold him still," said Ramsey.

There was more noise, more laughing, then Max said, "Okay we got him pinned. Rookie, we're going to give you a little shave."

I'd heard about rookies getting their eyebrows shaved. A team in Vancouver did that, but the players who did the shaving got in big trouble.

Kade was laughing again so I figured it wasn't his eyebrows. "Okay, let him up," said Ramsey. "He's done for now. Take the blindfold off and let him see what he has to drink."

"Gross!" yelled Kade. I deducted that he was actually enjoying himself.

"Let's do the Wong next."

I braced myself for what was to come. They pushed me to the floor so I was on my back. Someone was above my head pressing my arms down, and two others held my legs. Killer was on one, but I wasn't sure who was on the other. Hot Dog, perhaps? No, not him. The guy said something and I realized it was our goalie, Scott Brewster.

Pinned to the floor, I could do nothing when my shirt was ripped at the front, buttons popping off, bouncing on the floor.

"Hey," I yelled, "don't wreck my shirt!" I'd bought it with my own money just before coming to the school.

"I didn't get *my* shirt ripped," said Kade. "I just got my legs shaved."

"Don't wreck his clothes," said another player. I couldn't tell who it was, but it wasn't Ramsey, Killer, or Max. I wished I didn't have the blindfold on so I could see faces. I tried to breathe. Kade had only had his legs shaved. That was harmless.

"We can't do the same with everyone, otherwise a rookie party is no fun," said Ramsey. "Anyway, this rookie thinks he's tough on the ice and he thinks he's a player off the ice, so we're gonna see how much he can really handle. If he can stomach what we're going to do, I'll buy him a new shirt."

A player? I wasn't a player. I'd only ever kissed one girl.

What did Ramsey have in mind? I hated this. I wanted the blindfold off. I wanted this to be over. I had a horrible feeling in my stomach. None of this was me. I just wanted to play hockey. *It's going to be okay,* I told myself. *Stay tough.* I tried to breathe.

The razor grazed my chest. If this was it, I would be okay. I had little chest hair anyway. And it did tickle a bit, so I laughed. Kade had laughed and then they'd let him up.

"This is not it, Wonger." There was a strange excitement in Killer's voice.

"Let's not do any more to him," said Max. His voice was shaky. He was up by my head and had my arms pinned.

"No way," spat Ramsey. "Let's execute."

Hands were on my pants. My belt. My fly. I started to thrash and writhe. They couldn't do this to me. My foot hit someone. I kept kicking and punching and yelling for whoever it was to stop.

"Let him go!" Kade yelled.

"No. Keep him pinned down." Ramsey was fighting me, pulling at my jeans, dragging them and my boxers down my legs.

I kicked and kicked. "Let go of my hands, Max, please!" I begged. I had to cover my penis!

"Come on, Rammer," said Max, but he didn't let go of my arms. "He's had enough."

"I said pin him! Kurt, help Max with his arms."

The tension on my arms heightened. Pain ran through my muscles. Kurt had obviously joined Max, and they each had one of my arms, pressing their entire body weight on my biceps. By now I was spread-eagled on the floor, my pants down by my ankles.

Murmurs and mumbles erupted from the rest of the guys. Most were saying to let me go.

"What? Are you guys a bunch of fags? This is a rookie party!" Killer barked.

With Max and Kurt pinning my arms, and Killer and Scott on my legs, my thrashing lost its power even though I kept trying. I wanted to vomit. Ramsey pulled my pants over my feet. Now I wore only my ripped shirt.

"Keep him pinned," ordered Ramsey. Noise erupted from the room, shuffling and pushing and shoving.

"Someone hold Jensen back!" Ramsey yelled.

Suddenly the room took on an eerie silence. I could hear breathing, but the voices and the pushing and the shoving and fighting were over. What were they going to do?

I expected the razor to hit my skin. I thought they were going to shave me. I could handle this. I could. But the razor didn't come.

"We have to flip him over," said Ramsey.

Flip me over? Why? I wanted the blindfold off. "Let me go," I shouted. But they didn't let me go. I felt my body being dragged, lifted, and rolled until I was laying face down. They shoved me so my face was against the floor. Four guys held me there.

Nervous laughter spread through the room, the tittering type guys did when they looked at porn for the first time. What was happening?

Then I felt something hard and cold hit my butt. My

anus. A bottle? No way! This couldn't be happening. My heart raced, my body started convulsing. "No!" I screamed. "No!"

"Spread his cheeks!" Ramsey ordered. "I'm shoving this way up." I could feel the bottle against my skin, pushing inside me.

"You think you're good with girls," he hissed in my ear. "I think you're a virgin fag. I think you're gonna like this."

I went crazy. Like insane. I started thrashing wildly, using everything I had to get free, and then . . . someone let me go, let their hand slide off my wrist, someone who wasn't Ramsey. And suddenly I *was* free. I ripped off my blindfold and looked around. Max and Kade were holding Ramsey back, and Ramsey's face was purple and red, scary, his grimace full of hatred. For me. Why? I hadn't done anything to him.

"Let go of me!" Ramsey was yelling. "Let go!"

Max and Kade still held him tightly. His raging face became a blur. All the other faces became blurs too. I ran to the front door, picking up my jeans on the way, not even breaking stride to do so.

As I pushed open the front door and ran out onto the porch, I heard Ramsey laughing. Then I heard him say, "Hey. New nickname for Wong. Let's call him Wonger the Wanker. I think he liked it. Wonder what his girlfriend'll think of that."

No doubt he was making rude gestures as he said this, but I wasn't going to go back to see.

I slammed the door behind me, hurriedly put on my clothes, and ran. And when I say *ran,* I mean *ran.* My shirt flew wide open and I didn't care. My lungs felt as if they were going to burst, but I still kept running. When I reached the C-Train station, I finally slowed down. And then tears poured from my eyes. I didn't want to cry, but sobs shook me the way they did when I was a little kid. I punched the C-Train shelter wall. Then I kicked the stationary garbage can over and over.

A train was coming down the tracks, but I didn't make a move to get on it. Not yet. It stopped to let people on and off. I knew another one would be by in less than ten minutes. I'm sure I must have looked like a loser. Glad it was dark, I pulled my shirt together and held it sort of in place with the two buttons that hadn't been ripped off. I adjusted my jeans and did up the top snap. Then I wiped my eyes. I had to get it together and pretend like nothing had happened, at least until I got back to my billet house and into my bedroom. I glanced at my watch: 9:45. By the time I got back to my billet, Jordan would be in bed. With luck I could just slip downstairs without anyone seeing me.

"Hey." The voice was Kade's, right behind me. I hadn't heard him coming.

I refused to turn around.

"I brought your hoodie."

When finally I did look at him, I gritted my teeth. He looked like a dog that had just been caught with his face in the butter.

"I'm sorry, man. I tried to help." He handed me my hoodie. "I had no idea they were going to do that to you."

I took the hoodie and pulled it on, but only because

I was cold and didn't want to get on the train wearing a torn shirt. But I didn't speak. I know he'd tried to help, but he obviously hadn't tried hard enough. He'd been like everyone else in the room.

"Train's here," he said. "I'll go with you."

I shoved my hands in my pockets and looked away. "Go back to the party."

"No way."

"Your choice."

We boarded the train together.

I sat in a single seat.

# CHAPTER EIGHT

I didn't sleep well that night. Plagued by nightmares, I woke up exhausted and feeling like a piece of crap. I lay there in bed thinking maybe I should call it quits and go home to Vancouver. What would everyone think when they heard about this? I didn't want anyone to know, especially Carrie. Perhaps I could pretend it never happened.

But it did. Well, almost. I got away. At least I had that much.

*It didn't happen. It didn't happen.* I kept saying this over and over in my mind. Why me? Why had Ramsey chosen me? Was it because of Carrie? Or because I had stolen the puck from him in practice? Made him look stupid? Maybe he knew I got good grades and was jealous. That was easy to fix. I could purposely fail a few tests. But would that change anything? Not likely. My thoughts circled round and round.

I didn't want to go to school on Monday. And the idea of walking into the hockey dressing room almost made me throw up.

A knock on my bedroom door startled me. It had to be Jordan. He was the only one who'd dare knock on my door first thing in the morning. I glanced over and saw an eye peering at me through the open crack.

"Hey Jordan," I said.

As soon as he heard me, Jordan bounded into the room and jumped on my bed. "Breakfast is ready," he said. "Eggs and a smoothie."

"Thanks, buddy." I had to act normal.

"Did you have fun at your party last night?"

"It was okay," I lied.

"When's your first home game?"

"In two weeks."

"Do you have to go away next weekend?"

"Yeah." Nausea threatened again. Coach Rennert had told us that rookies would be roomed with the older guys.

"Come on, get up!" Jordan tugged on my blankets.

"Okay." Anything to get my mind off the rookie party.

Upstairs the smell of bacon and eggs greeted me, and my nausea was replaced by hunger. I'd hardly eaten anything last night. When I got home, I'd gone straight downstairs. I sat down at the breakfast table with Mrs. Dylan, Sam, and Jordan. Mr. Dylan was out of town on business and wouldn't be back until the next day.

This may sound odd, but there was a strange comfort in being with a family who hardly knew anything about me. If I was at home, my mother would have picked up on my mood and questioned me about the party. I would have yelled at her to stay out of my business, and then I'd be madder than I already was. But not here. Here it was easier because I could hide in anonymity.

"Do you have any plans for today?"

"I'll probably just study," I answered.

"Feel free to invite friends over if you want," said Mrs. Dylan. "Our house is your house."

*Yeah right*, I thought. *What friends?*

Mrs. Dylan passed around a plate of bacon. I took some and passed it on to Jordan who took the rest of the strips.

"Jordan took all the bacon!" wailed Sam.

"Give her some of yours, Jordan," said his mother.

I was grateful that the conversation about me was over. All the attention was on Jordan now, who was being silly and was showing off.

After breakfast I helped clear the table. Then I went downstairs to my room and closed my door. With my door closed, ostensibly so I could study, I could have privacy, and I needed it. Mrs. Dylan had made it clear to Jordan that when I was studying, he was not to bug me. I threw myself down on my bed and stared at the ceiling, letting last night run through my mind again like a skip in an old CD. How was I going to face my teammates? How was I going to go to school? The more I thought, the more agitated I became, and the more my hatred for Ramsey grew. How could I face anyone after what had happened?

Especially Carrie.

I quickly sat up and reached for my cell. What if Kade had told Carrie? My phone showed that I had two new messages, both from him. If he'd told Carrie what had happened to me, she probably wouldn't want anything more to do with me. I threw myself back on my bed. No, my best bet was to avoid everyone, go to practice on Monday, and just kick some ass.

I brooded on my bed for the rest of the morning and into the afternoon, trying unsuccessfully to get into the DVDs I was watching. I dozed and basically did nothing but feel sorry for myself. Around three my phone rang and I picked it up and looked at the number. Carrie. I groaned and closed my eyes. After the second ring, I thought I might as well get it over with. It would be better by phone, anyway. At least I wouldn't have to face her.

"Hello," I mumbled.

"Hi," she said cheerfully. "Do you still want to help me with homework? I'm totally stuck on question four."

"Um . . ."

She paused for a split second. "If you don't want to, that's okay." Her voice was quiet as if she was hurt I hadn't called.

Maybe Kade hadn't told her. She didn't sound as if she knew. I stalled for only one second before I asked, "Where do you want to meet?"

"Are you mad at me for Friday night?" she asked softly.

"No. I'm not mad at you."

"I'm sorry I got drunk. It was stupid of me."

"It's okay."

"You sure?"

"Yeah. Where do you want to meet?"

"I can come to your place," she said. "I've got a car."

"Okay, call when you're close and I'll come upstairs." I gave her the address. Then I got off my bed to take a shower.

Naked, I looked in the mirror. When I saw the bruises on my arms and legs, the horrible event played through my mind all over again. I turned away and stepped into the shower, letting the water stream over me. How would I have felt if they *had* shoved the bottle up me? Would I have been disgusted with myself? The physical stuff would disappear, but could I live with the memory?

When I turned off the tap, I heard Jordan outside the bathroom door. "Knock, knock. Someone's here to see you."

"Okay," I said. "I'll be upstairs in a minute." I grabbed a towel off the rack and wrapped it around my waist. I hoped Jordan had enough sense to keep Carrie upstairs until I was dressed.

My bathroom was across from my room, so I had to get to it without anyone seeing me. Opening the door a crack, I peered out, and seeing no one, made a bolt for my bedroom. I shut the door and got dressed in jeans and a long sleeved T-shirt. My shirt from last night lay in a crumpled heap on the carpet. I picked it up and tossed it in the laundry hamper. Then on second thought, I snatched it up and tossed it in the trash. I never wanted to wear it again.

I went up the stairs slowly, but when I hit the landing, I stopped in shock. Max stood on the mat by the front door.

"What do you want?" I faced him.

He tried to hand me a bag. A bag from a clothing store. I refused to take it.

"What is it?"

"A shirt."

"I don't want it."

"Hey, dude, sorry about last night." He shoved the bag in my hands.

If I didn't take it, I'd create a scene in the front hallway. I swung the bag back and forth, not really sure what to say.

"You won't tell Coach, will you?" Max whispered.

"No. I'm not a rat." I stared him in the eyes.

He looked away. "Rammer's got . . . issues." Then he said, "I gotta go."

I retreated back downstairs to my bedroom and threw the bag in the trash.

Carrie arrived ten minutes later, and this time I knew it was her because she called first, like we'd planned. Just seeing her in the front hallway gave me some comfort. She looked fantastic, her hair hanging long and kind of curled. I'd only ever seen her with her hair in a ponytail. She wore black leggings and a long shirt that was belted around the waist. She smiled at me like she did on Friday, but this time she wasn't drunk, so I was convinced she didn't know anything. I figured I might as well enjoy the day, my time with her, because news of the party could be all over school by tomorrow, and then she would hate me or think I was some sort of loser who had no balls.

"I guess we can go to my room," I said. "I have a work desk that's pretty big."

"Okay." She slipped out of her shoes and followed me downstairs. I didn't close the door because I wasn't sure how Mrs. Dylan would feel about me bringing a girl to my room. Trouble was not something I needed today.

"You have a great space," she said. "It's so big. The family I'm with have this little old war-style house, so my room is really small and I have a teeny tiny closet."

"Yeah, I'm pretty lucky," I said. "They bought this desk especially for me."

"So, do you like the hockey program so far?"

What to say? I had to keep this all neutral. "Practices are great. So is the dryland. I'm not sure about the yoga yet."

She laughed. "You guys do yoga?"

"Yeah. I can't do half the poses." I paused for a second, then said, "How long have you been at Podium?"

"It's my second year. But we have a lot of new synchro girls this year. Some were recruited and think they're pretty special. They're kind of catty." She played with her hair, twirling it around and around her finger.

*Okay, she was at the school last year.* My mind became clouded with thoughts. *Is that how she knows Ramsey? Did they go out?* I clammed up and couldn't speak, although I wanted to. I wanted answers. But if I asked questions, she might ask me about last night.

"Actually," she said with conviction, "some are just plain mean. I don't get them. It's why I like Allie. She's never mean. She's a great friend."

I opened my book. "Was she at the school last year too?"

"Yup. We met the first day and have been friends ever since." Then she groaned and opened her textbook. "We'd better get this done."

As I helped her through question four, showing her the proper steps to get to the answer, our shoulders occasionally rubbed. It happened again when we were finished, and she looked at me and smiled, her eyes crinkling in the corners. "Thanks for all your help."

"No problem." I swear I could feel her warm breath on

my face. And I definitely could smell her hair. I wanted to touch her. Feel her. After last night, I wanted to kiss her ... and prove that I liked girls.

But instead of making a move, afraid to make a move, I said, "You want something to eat? I could go upstairs and —"

"No!" she interrupted me. "I can't eat. I'm supposed to lose weight."

"You don't need to lose weight," I said. She looked darn good to me. Perfect, in fact.

"Ha ha. I'm in synchro. Have you not noticed how tall and skinny synchro swimmers are this year? Last year I was okay, but this year with the *new* recruits, I'm like way fatter than any of them."

"Yeah, but you're Curvy Carrie."

Her body went rigid and it looked as if a dark rain cloud had covered her eyes. "I bet Kade told you that."

"You don't like it?" I asked. It seemed like a compliment to me.

"I hate it." She almost spat the words. Tapping her finger on my chest, she said, "Don't call me that again." Then her eyes welled up with tears.

I suddenly got why she was upset. If people used *my* new nickname, and I was pretty sure the team would, I'd be upset too. For some really weird reason, I was almost glad that we shared similar stuff, because now I wasn't the only one. It made me feel closer to her.

I took her hand in mine. I didn't have the nerve to ask how she knew Ramsey. Not right now. I had other things in mind. "I swear," I said. "I'll never call you that again."

She looked directly into my eyes. I looked back. We were so close our noses touched. "You're sweet," she said.

*Sweet.* I didn't want to be sweet! I leaned into her. The feel of her body against mine felt good, so I pressed against her and put my lips on hers, kissing her hard, like, really hard.

"Whoa," she said, pulling away. She wiped her mouth. "Maybe we're moving too fast."

From the hurt look on her face, I knew I'd blown it.

What was wrong with me?

# CHAPTER NINE

The next morning, with my hoodie pulled up over my head, I stepped on the bus, found the first available seat, and took it. I didn't look at anyone, didn't say anything, and stared at the back of the seat in front of me. I couldn't even tell you who I was sitting beside. I thought I heard someone whisper "*Wanker.*"

A yoga class suited my mood perfectly, and when I entered the hot little studio, I found a spot in the far corner. Most of the guys were grumbling about yoga, but Rammer said, "Quiet, guys. It's good for core strength."

"Yeah, suck up," I muttered under my breath. He was just acting as if he liked yoga because he wanted to be captain.

In my little corner, I did all the poses halfway and I didn't give Ramsey the time of day, even though I knew he was sneaking looks at me.

When we got to the end of the class, however, and had to do the *savasana*, the pose where you just lie on the floor like a corpse, I listened to the instructor and closed my eyes. The instructor droned on about how we were supposed to let go of all thoughts, but for me that wasn't possible. I thought about school and how I was going to survive. Then I thought about Carrie. Why had I forced myself on her? And I still didn't know what had gone down with her and Rammer. She'd left pretty quickly after the kiss.

After yoga I was the first to shower and get on the bus. As soon as we pulled up in front of the school, I stood so I could be the first one off. As I walked toward the front doors, I heard Kade call my name, but I ignored him and went directly to physics, thankful that none of my teammates were in my class.

Carrie was already there, but she didn't turn to say hi. So I didn't say anything.

Allie plunked down in her seat, then stretched her long legs out in front of her. Her hair was so wild she looked more like a rock star than an athlete. Carrie whispered something to her and glanced at me, but that was it.

I heard a guy a few desks behind me say, "Hey, did you hear about the hockey rookie party? They really hazed someone!"

Heat spread through my body and into my face. I lowered my head and opened my books.

"Yeah, I heard," said another guy. "Who was it?"

"Not sure."

Allie turned around to get in on the conversation. "Man, that's so stupid, hazing," she said loudly. "Why do they do it? They give the school a bad name. What did they do this time?"

The teacher started talking then and saved anyone from answering. But I knew it was only a matter of time before everyone found out I was the one. For the rest of the period, I didn't look at Allie or Carrie and I didn't listen to the teacher either. Instead I planned my exit strategy from the room.

I watched the clock. I jiggled my leg. I put my hand on my leg to stop it from jiggling. I started tapping my pencil but stopped when I realized what I was doing. Finally class was over. And I bolted. It was my natural instinct I guess. With my head down, I went right by Carrie's desk and straight out the door.

Halfway down the hall, I heard her call my name. Then I felt her hand on my elbow. "Stop!" she said, panting from running.

"What?" I didn't look at her.

"What happened at the rookie party?"

"Nothing."

"You're lying."

I looked away.

"I have spare next period," she said quietly. "You want to go somewhere and talk?"

I didn't have a spare, I had English. But I replied, "Yeah, okay."

Believe it or not, I'd never skipped a class in my life. I was always afraid I'd miss something important, one small fact that would give me one more mark on an exam.

Outside we walked aimlessly down the sidewalk, heading in the direction of Subway. For half a block we said nothing. The leaves of the poplar trees were starting to turn golden already, and the sky was bluer and wider than I'd ever seen it. *The Alberta Big Sky,* I thought. I got that saying now, because the sky *was* big, not like in Vancouver, where mountains and large oak and willows hid the horizon.

"I'm sorry about yesterday," I blurted out.

Carrie took my hand. I squeezed her fingers.

"What happened at the party?" she asked.

"You don't want to know."

"Yes, I do."

"No, you don't."

"Yes, Aaron, I *do.*" She gently pulled my shirt to get me to stop walking.

So I stopped and turned to face her. "Why do you want to know?"

"It's important to talk about this kind of stuff."

"Maybe I don't want to talk about it. Maybe it's just too embarrassing."

"If you bottle it up, it will just eat you inside." She touched my cheek.

I put my hands up and stepped away from her. "Bottle? Do you think that's funny?"

"What?" She frowned in confusion.

"Why would you use *that* word?"

"It's just an expression. Why are you so mad?"

"You want to know what happened?" I kicked the ground with my foot. Then I looked at her and spat the words. "They tried to shove a friggin' bottle up me!" I knew I was bordering on yelling. "Is that what you want to hear? Who wants to hear something like that?" My body started shaking as I relived the event. "It's disgusting."

She put her hand to her mouth. "Oh, no! That's horrible!"

She moved toward me, took my hands, and looked me

straight in the eye, her gaze so compelling I couldn't turn away. "I'm so sorry."

"It's okay." I exhaled noisily. "I got away before it happened. I fought them off. So I guess it didn't really happen." I blew out another blast of air before I said, "I'm not gay. Ramsey wants you to think I am. But I fought like hell."

"Aaron, after yesterday, I know you're not gay. And just for the record, something like that would be torture for a gay guy too. It's sexual assault no matter who you are."

"Ramsey is an idiot. I don't know why he hates me so much. And some of the other guys went along with him like followers."

"Someone should stop him," she said.

"Whatever," I muttered. "But no one will."

"Talk to your coach."

"Yeah, right. Then everyone on the team will hate me. I'll have zero friends."

Just then a vision of Ramsey and Carrie together popped into my mind. "What's your story with him?"

"Nothing." She looked away.

"Hey, that's not fair. I opened up to you. Now it's your turn." I put my finger under her chin to guide her face back to mine. "Truth, please."

"Okay." She shook her head to get rid of my finger. I stepped back and crossed my arms, not liking her reaction.

"He tried to hook up with me at a party last year and I said no. He's hated me ever since."

"That's it?"

She nodded, then looked down at the ground. I didn't think she was telling me everything. I waited for her to continue, but she didn't, and when she finally looked up, tears ran down her cheeks.

"Aaron, I'm so sorry. I feel responsible for this. I think he was so mean to you to get back at me for not liking him."

"Hey, it's not your fault." I took her in my arms and hugged her.

She laid her head on my chest.

I stroked her hair. "Has he hated other guys you've gone out with?"

"I haven't gone out with anyone else." She pulled back just a little so she could look at me, giving me a quirky little smile and placing her hands on my chest. "I'm pretty picky. I have to really like someone. I don't just hook up with anyone, you know."

I pushed a strand of hair off her face, and electricity charged through me, a bolt so strong I felt weak but incredibly powerful both at the same time. "I don't either," I said.

"I like you, Aaron. I want to help you." She paused, then, "Are you going to do *anything* about it?"

"I'm going to kick their asses on the ice! That'll be my revenge." *Yeah. That's what I would do.*

My macho words made me feel like a macho man, so I drew her closer to me. "Can I?" I asked.

She smiled and moved against me. In the middle of the street, I kissed her softly, not at all like yesterday.

When we broke apart, we touched noses. Then she said, "We should head back soon."

"I'm starving," I said.

"All guys think about is food."

"Oh, I think about more than food," I said.

"Is that so?" she asked coyly.

"I'll buy at Subway," I said.

She scrunched up her face. "Nah. You can have my lunch. Let's go sit on the grass."

We found a dry grassy spot and sat down. I stretched out my legs; she sat cross-legged. Once again her lunch was an amazing sandwich piled high with cheese, turkey, and lettuce. "You get the best lunches. I get wraps that I can eat in two bites."

As I ate her sandwich, she munched on a carrot stick. In between bites, she said, "You should cut Kade some slack. He feels bad."

"You talked to him?"

"Last night."

"But you just acted like you didn't know anything."

"He didn't tell me what happened. He just said that some stupid things went down. When I asked what, he wouldn't talk about it."

I chewed, then took another big bite. The sandwich was exactly what I needed to fill something empty inside me.

"He tried to help, didn't he?" Carrie asked.

"*Tried* isn't good enough." I picked up a few blades of dried brown grass and threw them in the air. "I was blindfolded, so I didn't see much."

"If you were blindfolded, you couldn't see how he tried to help. So how can you be mad at him?"

"I guess I'm mad at everyone who was there."

"I hope we can all be friends again. It was fun at the

dance. I'm not much of a drinker, though. It's important to me to only drink with people I feel safe with, like Kade 'cause he's a friend from home."

"Yeah, it was fun." Suddenly I laughed, thinking about the dancing. "He and I were pretty bad dancers." I paused. "Okay, I'll give him another chance. I do need one friend on the team."

"Great! Because I think we should go on a double date with Allie and Kade — to a movie or something. They could be a good couple. They don't have to know it's like a date."

"Um, Allie and Kade didn't exactly get along the other night."

"So? Let's set them up anyway. How about this weekend? We could go to a movie, or to the mall, or even just Starbucks."

"The team leaves for Minnesota on Friday."

"Right. Okay. How about Thursday night? We'll have to check schedules."

"I'll talk to Kade."

"Promise?"

"Yeah, promise."

She stood up and brushed the grass off her legs, then gave me her hand so she could help pull me up. "Time for class."

I took her hand, but instead of letting her pull me up, I pulled her down. We wrestled on the ground, rolling around for a few seconds, our bodies close. She smelled like some kind of musk or flowers or . . . something that was really good, and her body seemed to fit perfectly with mine, especially her breasts as they pressed against my chest. Curvy, I liked. For a minute I forgot what awaited me back at school.

"Thanks for listening," I said.

"Any time."

"Just for the record," I said, "this was way better than English class."

# CHAPTER TEN

I'd missed an English pop quiz. It was worth marks too. I tried to tell myself I'd make it up somehow during the semester. English was a subject I did well in but not high nineties. This was the subject my parents gave me grief about.

I shouldn't have skipped class. But I'd needed to. Carrie had helped me through a tough time. Guilt can cause a lot of turmoil in your mind. My mind felt like a ping-pong ball, bouncing between what was right and what was wrong.

But by the end of the day, I'd convinced myself I might not have survived if I had gone to English class. And I still wondered about Carrie too. Had she been honest about Ramsey? Whatever. Her body against mine had felt great.

With my chin up and my gaze directed at no one, I walked into the dressing room. Rammer got up and stood in front of me.

"Well, if it isn't Wanker."

"Let it go, Rammer," said Max.

But Rammer didn't let it go and he got in my face.

Something brewed inside me, like a vat of poisonous gas. This was my chance, my chance to become a better hockey player, and I was not going to let someone like Tony Ramsey stop me. If I ran like a dog with my tail between my legs, I'd be ashamed of myself. But if I punched out Ramsey right now, then I was no better than he was. I wouldn't give him that satisfaction. Right now, I hated him. My talk with Carrie had given me strength.

I was going to fight this. I was going to slam him into the boards, slash him, spear him, and become a better player than him. I was going to work my butt off along the boards and take the puck from him. And if he wanted to fight, I'd do that too. I'd taken boxing in the summer; I knew how to throw a punch. But it would be on the ice.

And I was going to do everything I could to take his spot on the first line.

I pushed by him now, refusing to answer, tossed my hockey bag on the floor, and sat beside Kade.

"Hey," he said quietly.

"Hey," I replied.

I started to undress. No one else spoke to me. And I didn't speak either. I didn't hide my body with the purple bruises. Instead, I just went through my normal dressing procedure, putting on my under-gear, then my skates, jersey, and helmet.

I made sure I was dressed first and on the ice first. No more waiting at the door because I was a rookie. For the first time in a practice, Coach Rennert put us on lines, telling us, depending on how things went today, that these could be the lines for Minnesota. Killer centred the first line with Rammer and Max on the wings. Ben and I were put on the fourth line with Kade as centre.

Every shift, every play, every time it was my turn, I worked. I listened to the coaches and did everything they asked. We practiced the break-out, a lot, and then Coach Rennert made two power play lines, which I wasn't on. And he put together two penalty kill lines. I wasn't on them either.

*Don't give up. Don't give up. You will win if you keep working.*

Because of the type of drills we did during practice, I didn't get much opportunity to go against Rammer.

Until the end of practice.

"Okay, guys. You've worked hard today," said Coach Rennert. "Scrimmage for ten minutes. Stay with your line so you can get a feel for each other."

Rammer and his line went to one bench. "Follow me," I said to my line. Without even waiting for their answer, I skated to the opposite bench.

When I saw Rammer's line on the ice, I hopped over the boards. "Come on!" I said to Kade and Ben.

Kade jumped over the boards too, skated up beside me, and said, "Do you think this is a good idea?"

I didn't reply. I skated to the red line to get ready for the face-off.

I lined up against Rammer, and when the puck dropped, I shoved him hard. He shoved me back, but I was ready and held my balance. The puck skidded and Kade battled at centre for possession. When he managed to send it back to our defence, I charged forward, hoping for a pass. The puck bounced against the boards and I flew toward it knowing that I was offering myself on a chopping block for Rammer. At least that's what I wanted him to think. As predicted, Rammer headed toward me.

Speed. I had to use my speed. I got the puck on the end of my stick, played with it for a second until Rammer was closer, and fired it off the boards and up the ice. Then I used those first three strides I'd worked so hard on in the summer. Rammer crashed into the boards, missing me. I was long gone.

I skated to the puck, forechecking against Kurt on defence. Kurt was big and strong but not real quick. I moved with him behind the net. Yes, I was small, but I had nothing to lose.

I fought with Kurt against the boards for the puck. Rammer had dusted off and was now heading my way. *Good,* I thought. *Now he's out of position.*

I poked at the puck, shoving it to Kade. I saw Rammer coming toward me, so I braced myself. I put up my stick and Rammer hit it. He bounced off and came back at me. I thrust my shoulder into him. He hit back. While I hammered it out with Rammer behind the net, Kade took a shot and sunk it.

"You're minus one," I chirped to Rammer.

Every shift during the scrimmage turned into a battle between Rammer and me. I had no idea if Coach Rennert noticed, but that didn't stop me. I just kept fighting as hard as I could. Finally, when we were in a corner together, I slashed him hard, right on the top of the skates where there was little padding.

He threw his stick down and grabbed my jersey. I was

ready for him. He dropped his gloves and I dropped mine. He swung at me and I dodged him, just like I'd learned in my boxing lessons. I still wore a cage helmet because of my age, but he wore a visor, so I was in luck. He tried to grab my cage, but again I used my boxing moves to dodge him. Then I grabbed his visor and yanked off his helmet.

"Hey!" Coach Rennert yelled.

Suddenly I felt another body on my back. Killer. Then Kade jumped into the mix. Within seconds there was a big brawl on the ice and I had no idea who was on my side, but I didn't care. I wanted at everyone.

Coach Rennert skated into the brawl. "Enough!" he yelled. He started to separate us. Everyone suddenly stopped and we all looked at each other, realizing that this was crazy.

The Zamboni gate went up.

"No one undress," barked Coach Rennert.

I wiped the sweat off my face. I was done. Exhausted both mentally and physically, I went to the dressing room.

Coach Rennert came into the dressing room minutes after us. We were still in our gear.

"What the hell was that?" he shouted. Then he talked to us for ten minutes straight about respect. Disgusted with our behaviour, he kicked the garbage can on his way out.

I hung my head.

And yet, I wasn't really sorry.

# CHAPTER ELEVEN

Rammer didn't talk to me at all for the rest of the week, which was fine by me. I much preferred silence. I was a master at silence. I hated him, he hated me, but for the good of the team, we would forget and proceed. Or I would proceed and just take his spot on the first line. Fighting wasn't the way to go, but that didn't mean I couldn't get my revenge. From the dressing-room talk, I also knew Rammer had been to see Coach Rennert and he was thick with him.

Another good thing happened that week. Carrie got her wish and a double date was organized for Thursday night. Kade and I said we'd join them at the movie theatre after our practice and team meeting. I didn't have a ton of homework, although the English teacher had assigned an essay that was due on Monday. From what some of the guys on the team told me, we had study time on the week-end, so I figured I could get it done then.

In the dressing room after practice on Thursday, when we were all showered and dressed, Coach Rennert announced, "I've set the rooms for the weekend."

He passed out a room list to every player. When I read it, my stomach twisted into angry knots that just kept getting tighter and tighter. I was with Rammer and Kurt. I glanced up and saw Rammer staring at me with a cruel grin on his face. He'd orchestrated this.

"Sucks to be you," whispered Kade.

That night at the movie, I wanted to be in a good mood, but my stomach kept doing somersaults and drops off a cliff.

"What's the matter?" Carrie asked when we were leaving the theatre.

"Nothing."

"You're so quiet. Are you mad at me for some reason?"

I took her hand in mine and swung it back and forth. "It has nothing to do with you."

"Hockey stuff?"

"I have to room with Rammer this weekend."

"Are you kidding me?" Her voice had a weird quiver.

"Don't worry about me," I said. "I can handle him."

"I sure hope so," she said, then quickly added, "Allie and Kade are really getting along."

Why did she suddenly change the subject? Especially since there were clearly no sparks between Allie and Kade. Did it have something to do with me? Did she know something I didn't?

We arrived in Minnesota on Friday afternoon without any airline delays. I had never been to Minnesota and we were playing all our games at the arena at Shattuck–St.

Mary's, the school that Sidney Crosby had attended. There were eight teams in the tournament, and we were in Pool A with teams from Boston, Shattuck, and Notre Dame. Notre Dame College was in Saskatchewan, and had an amazing hockey program. I really wanted to go there in grade ten, but my parents had said absolutely not because it cost way too much.

As I lugged my bag up to my room, I kept telling myself how lucky I was to be on scholarship at Podium, and no one was going to ruin it for me. Our first game was later in the evening and I was pumped to play. I had been looking forward to this moment since I'd registered for the school last spring. We had one game tonight, two on Saturday, and one early Sunday morning. If we came first in our pool, then we would make the finals and play at two on Sunday afternoon. Our flight was for later Sunday evening.

We were each given a key, and when I opened my hotel-room door, I saw Rammer and Kurt unpacking their stuff. I stiffened. Being in a hotel room with Rammer scared the crap out of me. I swallowed and willed myself to act normal.

"You're on the floor," said Rammer.

"What?"

"There's only two beds, pal."

"I'll sleep on a cot or with Kurt. We're both rookies."

"No one wants to sleep with a Wanker."

I glanced at Kurt, who looked away. "You set this up," I said to Rammer.

"Yeah, I do have some pull with the coach. We're the only room with three. But he thought it would be a good idea for me to be with two rookies. He thought it would be a chance to bond and break down the barriers you seem to have put up."

I couldn't stand the pretend serious face he was making.

I threw my bag on the floor, picked up the phone, and punched in the number for Housekeeping. "We need a cot in room 616."

"They don't have any cots left," said Rammer, slapping his legs and howling like a monkey when he laughed. "I made sure of that."

I hung up the phone, unzipped my bag, and put my shaving kit in the bathroom. I finished organizing my things and without saying a word left the room. I could handle this petty stuff. It would make my revenge all the sweeter.

I hooked up with Kade downstairs in the lobby. We had a team meal before we headed to the arena to get ready for the first game of the season.

"So?" he said. I knew what he meant.

"I'm sleeping on the floor. Rammer asked for me to be in his room so he can make my life miserable."

"He feels threatened."

"And so he should. I'm taking his place on the first line, you know." The more I said it, the more I could make it reality.

"You're faster than he is."

"Yeah, but he's tougher, so I need to change that"

Kade's eyebrows shot up. "Not lately. You've been giving him a run." Kade paused. "He also hates you because Carrie likes you."

"Do you know what happened between them?"

"You don't?"

"A little. Tell me what you know."

"This is what Allie told me. Rammer tried to hook up with Carrie at a party. They started off talking and drinking. They both got a bit wasted and he got her into a bedroom. Jax Barren, a guy on the snowboarding team, walked in the room and saw Rammer on top of her on the bed. She'd been trying to fight him off but couldn't. So when Barren showed up, Carrie ran out of the room and the house with her clothes half off. Ramsey was so mad he punched a hole in the wall. No one said anything about it because the party had alcohol and they didn't want that known. Carrie didn't have another drink until the night we went to the dance. That's why Allie was so freaked out. But I guess Carrie thought because I was an old friend from home, she could let loose a little."

I nodded but didn't reply. I couldn't speak. Why didn't she tell me the whole story? I told her what happened to me. I sighed. So Rammer tried to force himself on her. No wonder she reacted the way she did when I kissed her last Sunday.

"He's a jerk," said Kade.

"We need to do serious damage this weekend," I said, changing the subject. I had to focus to achieve my goals.

"I'm totally psyched."

"Me too," I replied, gritting my teeth. I pushed Carrie to a bottom drawer in my mind and closed it tight. I had a hockey tournament to play and a first line to get on.

The moment arrived. I stepped on the ice wearing a maroon and gold jersey. We were told there would be NCAA scouts at this tournament. I skated hard in warm-up and focused only on hockey. Our first game was against Notre Dame.

When warm-up was over, I took my place on the bench to be the fourth line.

The whistle blew and I watched Rammer and his line. Then I watched the second line, the third line, and Rammer's line again. Halfway through the period, my line still hadn't played. The score was 0–0. The shots on net were six for us and eight for Notre Dame, a pretty even game so far.

Then Coach Baker, our forward coach, patted me on the back. "Get ready. Your line is out next."

We shuffled down the bench. My nerves tingled and my body was charged with electricity. The whistle blew, the gate opened, and I blasted onto the ice.

When the puck dropped, I moved. *Keep your feet moving. Keep your feet moving.* Ben picked up the puck on my opposite wing and started a rush. I skated with him. Key to scoring goals was driving to the net, getting in front, and moving constantly to get open. Ben passed the puck to Kade, and Kade rushed over the blue line. I swung behind him hoping for a drop pass. Kade saw me, made the pass, and I one-timed the puck. It pinged off the post and sailed behind the net. Ben rushed to the boards and Kade backed him up, so my job was to stay open in front. I kept moving my feet, back and forth, side to side, trying to dodge the Notre Dame defence and get in the open. He kept his stick on mine, holding me back. Kade tried to pop the puck in the net on a wrap-around, and a skirmish happened in front of the net, the puck still loose. The Notre Dame goalie tried to cover the puck but couldn't, and it remained free in front of the net. I poked and prodded and jabbed, hoping to get a garbage goal. But no luck. The goalie reached out and slapped his glove on the puck, just as I was sent flying to the ice by a Notre Dame defenceman doing his job well.

The whistle blew.

I looked up and saw Rammer's line coming out. I headed toward the bench. Coach Rennert said nothing to us, but by then I'd figured out he wasn't a coach who gave many positive compliments. But Coach Baker said, "Great shift, boys. Keep creating chances."

Once again, my line missed a rotation and sat on the bench. Nearing the end of the first period, we were given the go-ahead again. The score was still 0–0. If we could score, we could go to the dressing room with a lead.

Rammer came toward the bench waving his stick, tired and wanting off. I felt the push on my back. "Go!" said Coach Baker.

I jumped over the boards and raced to get into position. A Notre Dame forward had somehow picked up the puck in a turnover and was skating toward our zone. Max and Killer had lost the chance to get off the ice and had to stay out.

I pumped my legs to backcheck and catch the player with the puck. I gained on him, and when I was within one stride and he was ready to shoot on our goalie, I reached around and poked the puck free. It skidded toward the boards. I dove toward the puck, and as I was sliding, I swung at it and sent it to Max. Max took off with the puck down the ice. I got up and skated as hard as I could toward the other end of the ice, my legs screaming in pain when I crossed the centre line. To slow down in the neutral zone was a no-no, so I kept pumping, the lactic acid building.

I didn't catch up to the play before Max fired off a slapshot that zinged to the back of the net. Not thinking of anything but hockey and being on the ice during a great moment, I rushed over and joined the group hug.

"Great goal!" I said.

"You made it happen," Max replied. "Thanks."

I grinned. Forget about off the ice. On the ice was all that mattered.

At the end of the first period, the score was 1–0 for us.

In the dressing room, Kade said to me, "Hey, man, you got an assist!"

I shrugged. "More important, we're up."

Just before the ice was ready, Coach Rennert entered the dressing room to give his between-period speech.

"You have two more periods to go. It's still anyone's game. Keep driving to the net. That's the key. Get in front and get open." He looked at me. "Wong is doing a good job of getting open by moving his feet." Then he looked around the room. "Everyone has to work at that intensity every shift."

In the second period, our fourth line played in a regular rotation. We had chances to score but didn't. But then neither team did. At the end of the second, it was still 1–0 for us.

The third period started and the game suddenly went to a new level. Notre Dame came out hitting. Bodies crashed against the boards and fists flew, but no gloves were dropped. Coach Rennert kept telling us to play tough but not be stupid. Halfway through the third, no more goals had been scored, but there had been a lot of penalties. The whistle blew again, the ref pointed to Rammer, then made his motion. Two minutes for boarding.

Coach Rennert quickly scanned the bench. "Wong," he yelled, "Get out there!"

I hit the ice full stride. I was taking Rammer's place on the penalty kill!

We played the box and I was in the top corner. My job was to block any passes the Notre Dame defence tried to make to their forwards, or to block any slapshot that the D-man might make from the blue line. The puck went back and forth a few times from D-man to D-man. I skated with it, waving my stick, trying to make the Notre Dame D-man make a bad pass.

Then I saw him wind up. I got in front of him. I rattled him a bit, and he faked the shot and once again passed the puck to his partner. This time when he made the pass, I stretched but kept my balance, catching the puck with the tip of my stick and sending it out past the blue line. What happened next was all because Killer had muscle power and was an incredibly strong skater. He used his power and rushed to the puck, then he broke out and skated straight down centre ice, leaving the Notre Dame defence in shock. They pivoted and tried to catch him, but he was just too fast. When he was close to the goalie, Killer deked, pulling the goalie out of his net. Killer roofed the puck top shelf, and scored, short-handed.

We ended up winning the game 2–0.

# CHAPTER TWELVE

Curfew was immediately following our team meal. I trudged up to my room, tired but satisfied. For my first game with a new team, playing with guys I had never skated with before, I was happy with my work.

Only Kurt was in the room. I didn't know what to say to him, so I didn't say anything. From all his previous actions, I figured his loyalties were with Rammer and not me.

I pulled out my cell. The day before, I'd promised Carrie I'd call her after our first game. But for some reason, I didn't want to now. Maybe I was a little pissed off at her for not telling me the entire story about her and Rammer. Maybe I didn't want to be talking to her when Rammer walked in. I shoved my phone back in my bag.

I found a blanket and pillow in the closet and laid them on the floor in the far corner of the room. When I was done making my bed, Kurt pulled the cover off his bed and handed it to me.

"Thanks," I mumbled.

"No problem." He avoided meeting my eyes.

Once on the floor, I curled onto my side so the hardness wouldn't dig into my spine. I was actually drifting off to sleep when I heard the key in the door.

"You guys in bed already?" asked Rammer.

"Yeah," mumbled Kurt.

"I can see why *you're* tired," said Rammer. "But Wanker over there hardly played." He stood over me. "You should be thanking me for getting you on the penalty kill."

I rolled over and faced the wall. "Yeah, and I got two assists and you didn't get a single point."

"What'd you say?" Rammer barked.

"Leave him alone," said Kurt. "You got your wish — he's sleeping on the floor. I want to get a decent sleep so I can help *our* team tomorrow."

That night I didn't sleep much. I tossed and turned and just couldn't get comfortable. The more I couldn't sleep, the more agitated I got, working myself into a frenzy out of fear I was going to be tired all the next day and we had two games to play. I watched the red numbers on the clock flip and flip and flip. Finally, some time after three o'clock, I drifted off. Our alarm buzzed at six. We had an eight-thirty game.

Tired or not, I convinced myself I was going to play well. Our line played regular shifts. And we played decently, or at least Coach Baker told us we did after the game, which ended up in a 3–3 tie. My line didn't score, but we also didn't let in any goals, so we ended up with an even plus/minus.

Our between-games schedule had a designated study time, which we were allowed to take in our rooms. I made sure I got to the room first to get the desk. I pulled out my English books, started to do my essay, then, feeling the need to close my eyes for a minute, put my head down on my papers. Of course, with so little sleep the night before, I conked out. The next thing I knew, Kurt was shaking my shoulder.

I sat up. "Thanks," I said. Then I glanced around the room.

"He's in the can," Kurt said. He paused. "You want to sleep in the bed tonight?"

I shook my head. "I'm okay."

We lost our game that night 3–2. I didn't score, but I did get put out for the penalty kill a few times. All in all, I was playing okay. But okay wasn't good enough.

That night when I curled up on the floor, I fell right to sleep but then woke up at two in the morning. I groaned when I saw the time on the clock. I didn't want to be awake. I shut my eyes, willing myself back to sleep. But again I tossed and turned, throwing my covers off when I was too warm, then putting them back on because I was cold. My discomfort continued for almost an hour before I heard Kurt's voice.

"I'll move over," he whispered.

This time I accepted the offer.

I awoke hugging one side of the bed. Although it was better than nothing, four good hours of sleep was just not enough. How could I play well with so little sleep? My mind started to go to negative mode. Neither Rammer nor Kurt were awake yet, so I got up and padded to the bathroom to take a quick shower, hoping it would wake me up more.

"Thanks," I said to Kurt later, when we were leaving the room.

"I shoulda stood up to him," he said.

The lack of sleep did catch up with me and I didn't have my best game. That's what Rammer wanted to happen: break me down so I wouldn't have any advantage. In the third period, our line didn't play many shifts.

I sat on the bench, disappointed. Tired or not, I should have been better.

The game ended in a tie, which took us out of the medal round. We needed a win to be first in our pool, but we finished second out of four. Coach Rennert came into the dressing room for the post-game chat.

"We've got a lot of things to work on," he said. "But not bad for our first tournament. I think we have a lot of potential. But you have to work together as a team, on and off the ice. That will come. Get dressed. We'll go back to the hotel and check out. Since we don't have practice tomorrow, I'm going to hold a post-game meeting for each player in the afternoon. I'll email you with your time."

The day dragged. I mostly hung out with Kade.

Finally we got to the airport. I checked my bag but hauled my backpack with my books so I could do some homework on the plane. But when we hit the boarding gate, Kade asked me to go check out some of the shops and I agreed.

As we were looking at a rack of magazines, he said, "How's Carrie?"

"Dunno. Haven't spoken to her since Thursday."

He grinned. "That's a good thing. You're not whipped yet."

"Wanker and Carrie!" Rammer smacked me on the back. Neither Kade nor I heard him coming up behind us. "What a pair. One's gay and the other's frigid." Immediately, my hands balled into fists. Kade and I glanced at each other, and Kade shook his head as if to say, let it go. He knew I was ready to blow.

"I heard she's a little *fat* for synchro," mocked Rammer.

"Shut up." I snarled. "You're just pissed cause she turned you down."

"She didn't turn me down. She spread her legs."

"You lie!" Enough was enough. I wouldn't let him talk about Carrie like that. I pushed him. Hard. But not hard enough for him to lose his balance. He shoved me back. So I pushed again. Then he shoved me so hard that I toppled into the rack of magazines, knocking some to the floor. Kade grabbed at the magazines as I regained my balance to face Rammer, my fists up.

"You want to go? I'll go with you." He lifted his fist to slug me.

Kade pulled the back of my shirt. "Let it go," he whispered. "It's not worth it. The sales girl is on to you guys. She's got her hand on the phone. I bet she's calling security."

I jerked my arm, yanking away from Kade, and stormed out of the store. With my head down, and my mind churning, I bumped into someone.

"Sorry," I mumbled. Looking up, my heart almost stopped. I had walked into Coach Rennert.

"Sorry," I said again. Then I said, "Excuse me," and I veered around him, heading to an empty seat in the waiting area. My heart was beating in my chest like a lost bird flapping its wings in a winter storm. Standing up to Rammer was one thing. Getting in a fight with a *teammate* was something totally different.

I was out of control.

# CHAPTER THIRTEEN

I slept on the plane, instead of doing my English essay. When I got back to my billets', it was after midnight. Down in my room, I sat at my desk to do the essay. Two hours later, my eyelids drooping, my brain a puddle of soggy mush, I flicked off my desk lamp and crawled into bed. I curled under the duvet cover, hugged my pillow, and didn't wake up until my alarm went off.

Carrie wasn't in physics when I walked in the classroom.

"Hey," I said to Allie.

"Hi, Aaron. Kade said you guys did okay on the weekend. Okay, but not great."

So she'd already talked to Kade. I wonder what he'd told her. That I almost got in a fight? My mood sucked and I wanted answers from Carrie about her and Ramsey. I had to confront her. "I think we'd have had a chance if they had semis and finals. We came second in our pool." I kept the conversation going.

"I get ya. We lost too, by two points. We were so bummed. Especially since we outplayed 'em."

"Who'd you play?"

"A club team from Toronto." She turned in her seat to look at the back door. "I wonder where Carrie is."

A minute later, she waved and said, "Finally."

I turned. Carrie didn't respond to Allie's comment and there was no bubbly smile on her face. She slid into her seat and I heard Allie whisper, "What's wrong?"

Carrie shook her head and didn't turn around to face us.

After class, I waited for Carrie outside the classroom. Three minutes passed before she came out with Allie. Her face looked red and blotchy, especially around her eyes.

"I'll walk you to next class," I said.

"Okay." She barely smiled. Then she waved Allie on. "Thanks," she said. "Go, you're late."

Within a few strides, Allie was way ahead of us. Carrie and I started walking down the hall, and after a few seconds I asked, "What's wrong?"

"I hate catty girls."

I put my hand on her shoulder and stopped her in the hallway. By now it was empty as everyone had gone to class. She faced me and I looked her in the eye. I was going to say, "Tell me about it," but for some crazy reason, I blurted out, "Why did you lie to me about Ramsey?"

Her nostrils flared and her eyes took on this hard fiery look. "How can you ask me something like that right now?" Tears streamed down her face. "I just had the worst morning of my life."

"I just want an answer," I said quietly.

"Okay, I'll give you an answer." She threw her words at me. "I was drunk for the first time in my life. We had been talking so I trusted him. Then he forced himself on me. I felt like a slut."

I tried to take this in. I could picture Ramsey on top of Carrie. The image burned in my mind.

Carrie glared at me as if she knew. "See? I didn't tell you, Aaron, because I really like you. I thought you would think less of me."

"I don't think less of you. It wasn't your fault."

"It was. I stupidly got drunk. I stupidly thought he was my friend."

"But drunk or not, that's sexual assault," I said.

"You think I didn't know that? I had no idea what to do. And he didn't get to . . . finish, so there was no evidence." She flung her head back haughtily. "What happened to you was the same thing, you know. And you haven't done anything about it either."

She had a point. I hadn't done anything about it. No one from the team had. We were all trying to vacuum it up and seal it out of sight. "Hey, listen, I'm sorry. I'm sorry I asked about this now and I'm sorry he was such a jerk to you."

"You could have waited." Her shoulders drooped, all the anger dissipating, and her eyes welled up with tears.

"I just wanted you to tell me the truth." I lowered my voice. "I told you what happened to me and I thought you would do the same."

"It's not the same!" She paused for a second. Then she said, "There was one small difference in my case. What happened to me was my fault. I got drunk. I let him kiss me. But you did nothing wrong."

"Carrie, it still wasn't your fault."

"Shut up, okay? Just shut up. I don't want to talk about things that happened in the past. Ever. To anyone. I don't ever want to talk about this again."

By now she was almost hysterical, so I stepped closer to give her a hug and calm her down, but she pushed me away. "Don't!"

She turned and ran down the hall toward the girls' washroom.

# CHAPTER FOURTEEN

I walked into Coach Rennert's office at seven that evening for my post-tournament meeting. Coach sat at his desk. "Aaron, take a seat."

I sat across from him and sucked in a deep breath. My stomach churned as if it had crazy buzzing mosquitoes flying around inside it. Why was I feeling so nervous?

I guess the truth was, I really wanted to tell Coach Rennert about the rookie party. I had even practiced a speech in front of the mirror. That's why I was so nervous.

"I thought you played well on the weekend," started Coach Rennert.

"Thanks." The mosquitos stopped buzzing and I felt my shoulders relax.

"You're a good skater and you're tough. I like those qualities in a player."

He paused and I didn't say anything back.

"You need to work on positioning, though. Sometimes you're a puck chaser. You've probably always been fast, so you've developed the habit of always going where the puck is. With this team, I want you to focus on your positioning and my systems."

"Okay," I replied. I appreciated this comment. It gave me something to work on in practice.

"I also like your work ethic — it'll take you a long way. You keep working this hard and you'll find that opportunities to play on the penalty kill and power play will open up."

"Thanks," I said.

Then Coach Rennert leaned forward, lacing his fingers together, and stared at me, a stare that seemed to go right through me, causing me to almost hyperventilate.

"We do have something to discuss, though."

"Sure," I said, my voice barely a whisper. Did he already know about the party?

"How are you getting on with your teammates?"

"Good," I said too quickly. Why did I say that?

"I saw the pushing and shoving between you and Tony in the airport yesterday," he continued. "And you were heavily involved in the fight on the ice the other day at practice."

"I'm, uh, sorry about that, Coach." My prepared speech had vaporized.

"You can talk to me if something's wrong." He paused. "I try not to step in unless I think something is out of control, like the fight on the ice. I cannot have my team fighting each other. Because Tony is acting captain, I talked to him earlier and told him I've been concerned about some of the things I'm seeing between the two of you. He tells me he thinks you're a big asset to the team. That reassured me somewhat, but I wanted to bring this up with you, as well. Hear your side of things."

I swallowed. Tony had said something nice about me? Then I said, "Everything's fine."

"Good." Coach Rennert stood. He looked down at his list. "Tell Kade to come in."

I walked out of Coach's office in a daze. "Kade," I said, my voice shaky, "you're next."

He looked at me funny but then proceeded into Coach's office. The door shut, leaving me alone in the hallway. For a few seconds I stood still, trying to catch my breath, trying to figure this mess out. Why hadn't I said anything?

Because Ramsey had said good things about me. If I said something bad about him, I would've looked like a big baby.

I left the building. Mrs. Dylan was waiting for me in the van.

"How was your meeting?" she asked when I climbed in.

"Good," I lied.

"We saved dinner for you," said Jordan.

"Your mom called," said Mrs. Dylan. "She wants you to call tonight. She said she couldn't reach you on your cell."

"I had it turned off."

Mrs. Dylan grinned. "She wants to send you a care package."

A lump formed in my throat. I thought of my old team-mates, my old team, and my coach who put me on the first power play, a coach who liked me and how I played.

As soon as I got to the Dylans', I went down to my room

and phoned home. "How's school?" my mother asked.

"It's going okay." I lay on my bed, staring at the ceiling. I liked the sound of her voice.

"I'm sending you some food. I got some good things at the Chinese market."

"Thanks."

"Do you need anything else?"

"No, I'm okay."

"I'll let you talk to Dad," she said. From the noise I could tell she was handing over the phone.

"Hello, Aaron," he said. He actually sounded jovial, as if he had telepathy and knew he had to cheer me up.

"Hey Dad."

He asked all the same questions my mom asked, except he grilled me on the school stuff a little more. "Your English teacher sent an update today," he said.

"Oh yeah."

"You missed a quiz. It counts for marks."

"Yeah, like point zero-zero-zero five."

"Why did you miss?"

"I was at the guidance office straightening out a few things," I lied. "Don't worry. I'll get that mark up."

"Remember, ninety-five percent on every subject or you come home."

"I know."

"Do you need any sticks?"

For the first time that day, I laughed. My dad never asked me if I needed sticks. I always had to ask first and he always made a big stink about how much they cost and why I couldn't just use a wooden stick that cost twenty dollars.

"Sure, if you're buying," I said. I waited for the lecture about money and how if I was to play hockey, I'd have to pay for everything myself.

"Tell me what kind and I'll get them for you. Send me an email."

"You got a deal, Dad."

"Your mom and I want to visit you next month and see one of your games. I'll bring the sticks then. And I'll visit your English teacher."

This was a bit of a shock. I honestly didn't think I'd see my parents until Christmas. "That'd be great," I said. And I meant it too. "How's Erica?"

"She's good. She's at music lessons right now."

"Tell her I said hi and I'll call her later. Maybe we can Skype."

"She would like that. She says it's too quiet here without you."

When we hung up, I snapped my phone shut and placed it on the night table, then curled up under the duvet and fell asleep.

I awoke at midnight still dressed in my jeans and T-shirt. Darn. I hadn't done my homework either. I sat up, rubbed my face, and went to my desk. I managed to get my homework done in an hour, but when I slipped back under the covers, it took me another hour to get to sleep. My alarm went off four hours later.

# CHAPTER FIFTEEN

Carrie avoided me the next day. I hated it. I didn't want her to avoid me. Every time I saw her or passed her in the hallway, my heart picked up speed and my sweat glands opened. She made my heart ache. How sad is that?

She definitely was more complicated than I originally thought. But that didn't scare me. In fact, it made me like her even more.

I went to practice, worked hard, ate dinner, then went down to my room to do my homework. Only, I couldn't concentrate on my homework. I fiddled with my cell and finally, when I could stand it no longer, I sent Carrie a text. "Can we talk?"

When I heard the familiar beep, I quickly picked up the cell and read the word "sure."

I phoned her immediately.

"Hey," I said.

"Hey," she said back.

"I'm really sorry about yesterday," I said next.

"It's okay. I'm sorry for not telling you about Ramsey. I used to feel badly for him, but not anymore. He's a jerk.

Anyway, I didn't tell you because I didn't want you to think less of me."

"Why would you feel anything for him?"

She waited a beat before she said, "Uh, family crap. His dad left him and his mom high and dry when he was a baby. Then Tony became good at hockey and his father wanted back in his life, thinking he was going to the NHL. Such a jerk. He doesn't love him. He just loves that he might be an NHL star."

"I heard a bit about that. Well, just that his father left." I paused. "I didn't, you know."

"Didn't what?"

"Think less of you."

"I guess I should've known that but . . . we've only been hanging out for a week."

"Do you think we're moving too fast?" I sure didn't think so, but who knew with girls?

She laughed. "Aaron, we're not even officially going out yet and I think we had our first fight. That's crazy."

I laughed along with her. "Yeah, it is." I paused. "Should we slow down? Is that what you want? Just hang out for a while?"

"Sure. Maybe that's best."

All week Carrie and I pretended we were just friends. We hung out at school and talked at night, but we didn't get close physically. That part I hated. I wanted her near me. And all week I tried to stay away from Rammer and Killer. If I saw them in the hall at school, I went the other way. I never sat beside either of them in the dressing room and

Coach Rennert didn't allow us any scrimmages in practices, so I didn't have to go against them on the ice. I buried the rookie party. But I didn't bury my goal to get on the first line. Time would dictate my success.

All seemed to be going okay, and by the end of the week, I was even starting to sleep a little better. We had a physics test on Wednesday and I knew I aced it. We had a home game in Calgary on the weekend and I couldn't wait to play, especially since Allie and Carrie were coming to watch.

Before practice on Friday, Coach Rennert walked into the dressing room.

"Listen up, guys," he said.

We all stopped what we were doing and listened.

"I've chosen the captains for the rest of the season," he said. "Ramsey will wear the C. Kilby and Max will be alternates. One of Ramsey's jobs will be to relay information from me to you. I expect you to listen to him."

Practice was light, not much skating, but a lot of positional play, just what I needed. I was still on the fourth line with Ben and Kade, and I wondered if I would ever get moved. I had to. I just had to. And I would because Coach Rennert had me practice a bit on the power play. That meant he was starting to trust me.

We all hit the showers afterwards and the mood in the dressing room seemed upbeat. I had just come out of the shower when Rammer said to me, "I forgot to tell you. Coach wants to see you as soon as you're dressed."

My blood raced and I suddenly felt hot. Had I done something wrong?

"Do you want me to wait for you?" Kade asked.

"Sure," I said. "I doubt I'll be long."

"Yeah." Kade chuckled as he tossed his elbow pad in his bag. "Rennert isn't known for his long speeches. If he gives you two words, you're lucky." Coach Rennert was standing outside the door when I walked out. I went over to him and dropped my bag.

"Good," he said. "Ramsey remembered and you listened to him." Without so much as a breath, he continued, "If you play well this weekend, I might use you on the power play. I'm keeping you with Kade and Ben, because I need you to lead the line."

I nodded, stunned and thrilled.

Coach patted me on the back and without another word walked down the hall. I picked up my bag. As promised, Kade was waiting for me in the lobby.

"So?" he said.

"Nothing bad. He might use me on a power play."

Kade grinned and slapped my back. I knew he wished he was the one to get the good news. "You're next," I said. "We're still on the same line and we're going to score this weekend."

The entire Dylan family and Allie and Carrie came to watch my game on Saturday night. It was exciting to have a few fans in the stands, and I honestly looked forward to the day my parents came and watched me play. They were even going to let Erica skip a music lesson so she could come to Calgary too. I sort of liked it that they missed me.

First shift out, our line was on fire. Kade hit the post, I

zinged the crossbar, and Ben set up both shots with perfect tape-to-tape passes.

"Good shift," said Coach Baker when we came off the ice.

"Let's keep it up," I said to Kade and Ben.

Next shift out, I lined up at the face-off. Kade was going to send the puck back to our defence and I prepared to break out. The puck dropped and Kade won the draw. I flew up the ice, and when the puck hit my stick in a perfect pass, I pumped my legs. The opposing defence tried to angle me into the boards so I did a fake, catching him flat-footed. Ben skated with me. We had a two-on-one!

Once over the blue line, I flipped the puck to him and he rifled a shot on net, hitting the goalie's pads. The puck rebounded out front and I picked it up, eyeing Kade, who was hovering around the post. If I could get it to him, he would have a wide open net, but I would have to lift it slightly to get over the sticks in front of the net. I backhanded it.

Sure enough, Kade snapped at it, tucking it into the top corner of the net. His arms went in the air when he realized he'd scored.

I immediately skated over to him and, along with the rest of the line, we group-hugged. Our team was on the scoreboard. Our line had scored.

The first period ended with the score at 1–0. When we left the ice to go to the dressing room, Jordan and his friend were hanging over the glass. "Hey Aaron!" he yelled. "Give me a high-five!"

I slapped his hand but didn't break stride.

The game heated up in the next period. The ref called

a lot of penalties, trying to get the game under control and stop anyone from fighting. When Rammer got sent to the box for his fifth penalty of the game, Coach Rennert shook his head, then looked up and down the bench. I held my breath. *Please,* I thought, *call my name.*

"Wong," he said, "go."

*Yes!* I hopped the boards and took my place on the penalty kill. I did my job, managing to clear the puck twice, and after a minute of play, came off. Coach Rennert didn't say anything, but Coach Baker patted my helmet. "Good job."

That period we played twelve of the twenty minutes short-handed. They scored two power-play goals to take a one-goal lead.

Coach Rennert stormed into the dressing room between the second and third period. "Next guy who takes a dumb penalty sits!" He turned on his heel and left the room. No one said anything for the rest of the break.

Just before we headed back out, Rammer stood and said, "Let's get the goal back. No backing down. Hit them hard. We can win this."

The period started off okay. Kade, Ben, and I almost scored again. Coach Rennert rolled all four lines and we just kept taking our shift, thankful he wasn't shortening the bench and making us sit. Halfway through the third period, Rammer's line was out. The face-off was in the opposition's end. Killer won it and sent the puck back to Kurt on defence. Kurt took a look, then passed to Rammer along the boards. Rammer picked it up, tried to move the puck, but was slammed against the boards. He pushed back. The guy shoved him again.

The ref yelled, "Play it."

A tough contender, Rammer managed to win the battle, then looked up and fired the puck to Killer, who was behind the net. Then Rammer zipped to the front of the net. Killer fed him a pass and he took a shot. It hit the goalie's pads and rebounded out front. Sticks poked and prodded around the goalie, who was trying to get his glove on the puck to freeze it. Rammer got the puck and tried to take another shot, and as he did, he pushed the goalie. The opposing defence didn't like this at all, and the pushing and shoving started.

Rammer grabbed the jersey of the player who pushed him. The guy tried to punch Rammer. Then Rammer did the ultimate and dropped his gloves. The refs flew into the battle, but the gloves were already off both players. Rammer punched the other guy and was punched back. The refs tried to stop the fight, and after a few more punches were thrown, Rammer and his opponent were sent to the dressing rooms.

Rammer chirped at the other player all the way off the ice. He was out for the remainder of the game and probably for the next game too. Dropping the gloves and fighting was an automatic game suspension.

Coach Rennert called my name. "Wong, you play with Killer and Max."

I had my chance!

My first shift out, I skated hard but barely touched the puck. Max passed to me, but Killer never did, even when I was wide open. What a jerk! He was trying to make me look bad. Skating off at the end of the shift, I wondered if Coach Rennert would pull me off the line and try someone else.

I waited, but I wasn't told to play on another line. I made up my mind that next shift would be different and I would win the trust of Killer.

The line change was on the fly, and when it was my turn, I flew. Killer had the puck and was rushing forward. I skated harder than ever, blasting up the ice, keeping pace with him, pushing myself to my max. We both went over the blue line and I got myself open to accept a pass, but he shot on net. The goalie made the save and we regrouped for the face-off. This time I got the puck on my stick. Max wasn't open, but Killer sure was. I saucer-passed the puck over the opposing defenceman's stick, and when it landed right on Killer's stick, he one-timed it, hitting the back of the net.

We had tied the game.

With four minutes left, the score was still 2–2. I looked up at the clock. At best, I had only a few shifts left, especially if Coach Rennert continued to roll the lines. Then the whistle blew. Kade had drawn a penalty; we would now go on the power play.

"Wong, Max, Kilby, get out there."

My first chance on the power play! I exhaled and skated to my wing. *Stay in position,* I told myself. The key to a good power play was to keep the puck moving and get in the right position to score. Killer won the face-off and sent the puck back to Kurt. I moved to the boards. He passed to me and I quickly sent the puck to Killer, who was now behind the net. He passed it back to me. I looked for Max, but he wasn't open. I flipped it back to Kurt, who sent it across to our other defenceman. The puck cycled around for a few more seconds before getting back to Kurt. The second he wound up for a slapshot from the point, I rushed in and lifted my stick in the air. The puck deflected off my stick, changed directions, and landed in the back of the net. The goalie didn't have a chance.

Kurt rushed over to me. We hugged and Max joined us. Killer skated to the bench to accept the glove-to-glove accolades. Skating back to the bench, I snuck a quick glance to the stands, hoping to see Carrie. No such luck. Then I saw Rammer in the stands with some older guy. They were both staring at me. Was that his dad?

Under my helmet, I smiled.

Revenge was so sweet.

# CHAPTER SIXTEEN

"Awesome game!" said Carrie, beaming. "You scored the game winner."

"Thanks." I dropped my bag and leaned on my stick.

Allie grinned and pretended to box. "You gotta love the fights in hockey."

I laughed. Kade grinned and jerked his head toward her. "She's crazy."

"Hey," said Allie, "are we still going for pizza? I'm starving."

"Yeah," I said. "Let me talk to the Dylans first and tell them where I'm going."

"Jordan is going to be so excited that you scored the winner." Carrie laughed. "I think you're his hero now."

And Jordan was excited. He gave me a huge high-five that almost knocked me over, and the Dylans congratulated me over and over again. It felt good to have such support.

After I said goodbye to the Dylans, the four of us went to Boston Pizza, and we laughed and talked about everything and anything. My elation lasted all evening. Carrie and I made a lot of eye contact across the table. We had hung out all week and I definitely knew that I wanted more than just hanging out.

So when our feet touched under the table, I didn't move my leg. And neither did she. Then when Carrie seductively rubbed my shins with her bare foot, I grinned at her. Two weeks was more than enough time. It was time to put the moves on again.

Monday afternoon I entered the dressing room full of energy. I'd finally caught up on my sleep. And I'd gotten ninety-six percent on my physics quiz, but only ninety-two on the English essay. Bummer. I hoped my dad wouldn't find out. But the English teacher had moved us to a novel study, and I had already read the book, so it would be a cinch to get a good mark.

On the ice, Coach Rennert called out the lines. Kade, Ben, and I were now on the third line, which was okay with me. We had played well together and received a lot of ice time, and for a few minutes, I had Ramsey's spot on the first line. I was convinced that I would have that spot permanently if I just bided my time and kept working my butt off.

Halfway through the practice, Coach Rennert called me and Ramsey over. "Change places for the rest of the practice. Wong, you'll be playing with Killer and Max. Ramsey, you're out next game."

I heard Ramsey swear under his breath as he skated over to Kade and Ben.

As much as I liked playing with Kade and Ben, playing

with Max and Killer was a new level of hockey. Sure, I was a quick skater, but these guys were quick with the puck. I had to force myself to read and react.

By the end of practice, I was drenched. I threw my sweat-soaked gloves in my bag.

"I wouldn't get too comfortable," said Killer. He was sitting beside me in the dressing room. Kurt was on my other side. "Rammer will be back."

"Maybe," I replied curtly. I continued to unravel the tape from around my shin pads. He didn't say anything else. After Killer hit the showers, Kurt said, "I thought you did pretty good out there today. I think you're better than Rammer."

Man, that felt good! "Thanks," I said.

With my towel and shaving kit, I went to shower. Rammer and Killer were coming out when I was going in, and I stepped aside to let them by, wanting no trouble.

"So, Wanker, you still wanking Curvy Carrie?" Rammer hadn't called me Wanker in a week.

"Shut up."

He grabbed my shoulder and shoved me against the wall. "I asked you a question. I'm the captain. Answer me."

"I don't have to answer that question." I pushed him off me. "It has nothing to do with the team."

He snickered. "She's as cold as a dead fish."

Heat rushed to my face and I moved in so my face was close to his. "She doesn't go for *losers* like you. You tried, remember? She didn't want you."

"Loser?" He spat the word. "You calling me a loser?"

"What else would you call it when a girl dumps you in front of a crowd of people?"

"One of these days, I'm going to finish what we started at the rookie party. Only you won't know when that'll be. Could be Christmas. Could be March. You'll never know."

From nearby, Max said, "Rammer! Relax, dude."

"Take a chill pill, Rammer," Hot Dog chimed in. "Or better yet, eat a hot dog!"

Everyone laughed, or tried to laugh, and the moment was over. Rammer moved out of my way. I lifted my hands as if to surrender and headed into the shower. Under the streaming water, my body shivered. Was he serious? Was he really going to get me back?

At least the guys had stuck up for me this time. Perhaps with their support, over time he would leave me alone for good.

I was still dressing when Rammer and Killer were leaving. At the door, Rammer turned and said, "Oh, Wanker, I forgot to tell you — Coach Rennert wants to see you."

I eyed him for anything suspicious, but there was nothing there. Maybe Coach wanted to talk to me about being on the first line next game. Maybe he had something he wanted me to work on. That made total sense. No way Rammer would make good on his threat right away. I knew him. He'd make me sweat.

Obviously seeing my hesitation, Rammer held up his hands. "Hey, I'm Captain and Coach wants to see you. I wish he didn't, but I'm supposed to tell you and you're supposed to listen. End of story. I will get my position back, though." Then he left, with Killer following.

I exited the dressing room and searched the hall for Coach Rennert, but couldn't find him. He wasn't in the front lobby either. There was a back office that he sometimes used. I headed there. The bus driving us home from practice would be leaving soon. I hoped Coach had told the driver to wait.

When I got to the back office, no one was there and all the lights were off. When I turned to go back to the lobby, Rammer and Killer were coming down the hallway. "Drop your bag, *loser,*" Rammer snarled.

My heart raced and my body got sweaty and clammy. Had I walked into something!

"What do you want?" I asked. "Where's Coach Rennert?"

They grabbed my hockey bag off my shoulder and threw it to the floor. Then they pushed me toward the fire exit. Within seconds I was outside in the freezing cold and the pitch-black night. And we were alone. This exit was at the back of the arena, away from the parking lot and away from lights and people. They both shoved me against the concrete wall. How could I have been so stupid?

"I told you I'd get you when you least expected it," hissed Rammer. "I bet you didn't think it'd be right away. Don't ever call me *loser* again."

His face was inches from mine, and in the dark I could see that his eyes were glazed over as if his anger were sitting on his skin instead of inside his body. His warm breath hit my face like a furnace on high and I turned my head.

Then he kneed me in the stomach. I doubled over, gasping for breath. I reacted by trying to take a swing. But

Killer grabbed my arm and Rammer punched me in the stomach, the blow knocking the wind right out of me. Once again I doubled over. My vision started to blur.

Rammer pushed me hard and I lost my balance, falling to the snowy pavement.

He kicked my side. I tried to get up and crawl away, but they had me cornered. The toe of his boot dug in the area just above my hip. Finally I curled into a ball to protect myself. I could do nothing else at this point. It was two against one.

"That's enough," said Killer. "He's cowering like a baby."

Rammer bent over. "I'll be back on the line next week and everything will go back to normal. And remember, I didn't hit you. You can't prove I did anything to you. No one witnessed this. It was to show you your place. You tell Coach Rennert or anyone, and I'll make sure you get kicked off the team and out of the school. He'll believe me, not you."

Then he held out his hand to help me up. "No hard feelings."

"Fuck you," I said.

He kicked me one last time before they left me alone.

# CHAPTER SEVENTEEN

I lay curled up on the ground for a few seconds before I tried to get up. My side ached. When I tried to stand, I slipped but grabbed the wall. I inhaled and exhaled, trying to get myself back to normal so I could face the rest of the guys. I didn't want anyone to know anything. I re-entered the hallway by the fire exit, grabbed my hockey bag, and slowly made my way down the hall. When I reached the lobby, I was alone. Everyone was gone. The bus too.

*Damn.* I got out my cell phone and punched in Mrs. Dylan's cell number.

"Aaron," she said.

"I missed the bus. Can you pick me up?"

"Oh dear. How did that happen?"

"I just got held up."

"Not to worry. I'm picking up Jordan now so I'll swing by and get you.

I waited outside, and in a way I was glad I missed the bus. I didn't have to talk to any of the guys and pretend like nothing had happened. When Mrs. Dylan pulled up in front of the arena, I could see Jordan waving like crazy, his face pressed against the glass.

"Aaron," he said as soon as I climbed in the minivan, "I scored five goals in practice today!"

"That's great!" I said. I patted his back, and the movement made my side ache.

"How was practice?" Mrs. Dylan asked.

"Good." I tried to sound normal.

For the rest of the ride, Jordan stole the conversation. When we got to the house, I excused myself and went to my room. Once there, I sat on the end of my bed, still stunned by the beating. Did it really happen to me? I pulled up my shirt and saw the redness on my side where Rammer had kicked me. My skin felt really sore and tender. When I touched it, I winced. I was sure it would be bruised by tomorrow. Coach Rennert told me to talk to him if anything was wrong. Something was wrong. That much I knew.

After dinner, I took two pain-relievers. Mrs. Dylan gave them to me when I told her I had a bad headache. I fell asleep on my bed with my English books open. I woke up when my phone rang. My home number lit up the screen.

"You aren't keeping your marks up," said my dad.

"What are you talking about?" I closed my eyes. I didn't need this now.

"We got another English update. This teacher is good. She sends one every week. You only got ninety-two on an essay."

"Don't worry!" I snapped. "That mark is easy to pull up."

"What are your other marks like?"

"They're good."

"You sound too tired to do schoolwork."

"I'm fine. By the time you come, my marks will be great."

"Your mother misses you," he said before we hung up.

I awoke again in the middle of the night, and when I got up to go to the bathroom, I became aware of how sore my side was.

I was groggy. I didn't even turn on the lights when I went to the bathroom. And when I was back in my room, I tossed my English books on the desk, took another two pain-relievers, and went back to bed.

Fortunately we had yoga in the morning, not dryland. With yoga I could stand in the back and pretend to do the exercises. When the lights were off at the end of class, I kept thinking about what I was going to do, how I would handle this. I hadn't told Carrie yet and maybe I wouldn't. I made it through yoga and sat beside Kade on the bus. We didn't talk.

Kade and I walked into school together. "What happened to you last night?" he asked when we were alone. "You missed the bus."

"I had to talk to Coach."

Kade's forehead furrowed so his eyebrows were almost touching. I looked away hoping he would drop this conversation. "Rennert left before we did," he continued.

"I was talking to Baker," I lied.

"Nice try. He left with Rennert."

I had to change the subject. "Did you get your English done?"

"I don't have English this term." He paused. "Where did you go after practice? Something's up and you're not telling me."

"It's none of your business. Let it go."

Physics was boring and the teacher's voice sounded like a tire with a slow leak, one big hiss that just kept going and going. I tried to rid my mind of Rammer's boot kicking me, but every few minutes I put my fingers on my side to feel the tenderness and was instantly reminded. Should I tell Coach Rennert? The thought of ratting out my team-mates was more than I could stomach.

"Aaron." Carrie touched my arm. "Wake up."

Startled, I jumped in my seat.

She laughed. "Did you fall asleep?"

I picked up my books and acted nonchalant. "Of course not."

"Did you hear him say we have to hand in our home-work tomorrow for marks?"

"Yeah." I hadn't heard that of course, but I was sure glad she told me.

She took my hand, squeezed my fingers, and smiled coyly at me. "Will you help me with *my* homework? I can come over tonight. I'm done practice at six."

For the first time since yesterday, I smiled, a real smile. "Sure."

I made it through school and practice, although practice was hard and my skating was off because of the pain in my side. I tried not to let Coach Rennert know, and skated as hard as I could. Rammer said nothing to me and I said nothing to him. Killer also avoided me, although he did pass the puck to me once. I knew Coach Rennert wasn't thrilled with my practice. I wanted to tell him I wasn't feeling well, but he would ask what was wrong. There was no way I wanted to look like a rookie baby. After practice, I noticed that my pee was really, really dark and red and wondered if that had something to do with why I felt so tired. If I ignored it all, perhaps it would go away. I just needed some sleep.

When Carrie bounced into my room that night, the fragrance of her perfume, coupled with her infectious smile, made me feel a whole lot better. My billets were out, so we were alone in the house. "You smell so good," I said when I hugged her. She leaned her head against my chest and I nuzzled my cheek into her soft hair. Then she lifted her face. Our lips met and we kissed, a long, long kiss that made my body react. Man, she felt good. She was just what I needed to make me forget about Rammer. I was telling no one what he'd done until I figured out when — and if — I'd tell Coach Rennert.

After we broke apart, she giggled and pulled me onto my bed. I fell beside her and everything was going well, like really well — I even had my hand under her top and her bra and the softness of her skin and breast made me groan in pleasure — until she rolled over to get on top of me and her belt buckle pressed into my side.

"Ouch!" The pain made me yelp like a dumb dog.

"What's the matter?" She sat up, readjusting her clothing.

My body deflated. How could I have just wrecked the moment? "Nothing," I said.

I sat up too, even though I didn't want to. My face was hot with embarrassment and my body was hot because Carrie was hot.

"Are you hurt somewhere?" She stroked my chest with her fingers.

"Not really."

"'Not really' isn't really an answer. You either are hurt or you're not."

I smiled and kissed her fingers. I wanted to tell her but couldn't. "I've just got a bit of a sore side from a hit today. Let's go back to where we were."

"Let's do our physics first, then . . . we can have some fun later." She seductively raised her eyebrows.

We worked hard and got our physics homework done, and Carrie even *understood* the work, which made our studying time speed by, giving us more time for fun.

"Let's watch an episode of *Friends,*" she said. "We can snuggle under the covers." She smiled seductively, or at least it looked seductive to me, so I pulled back my duvet.

She grabbed season one from my pile of DVDs. "I'm so glad you like this show too. I love the early shows. They wear such bad clothes and their hair is hysterical."

"Yeah, and Joey is funny. Put it on and I'll go upstairs and get us something to drink."

"No snacks," she said. "And no juice. Just water or Diet Coke for me."

I walked up the stairs. I tried to run, but the pain in my side was bugging me. I couldn't figure it out why it hurt to touch and ached when I moved too much. It seemed to be getting worse rather than better. And I had absolutely no energy. I found a diet drink for Carrie and some juice for myself and brought the drinks back downstairs. Carrie and I snuggled under my covers to watch television. I was wearing my sweats, and within ten minutes, I was so warm I thought I was in yoga class. I said so to Carrie.

"Take off your clothes," she said, "if you're that warm." She giggled. "You do have boxers on, don't you?"

I whipped my sweats off, throwing them on the floor. "Yes, I have boxers on."

She laughed and put her hand to her mouth. "They've got cows on them!"

I tossed a pillow at her. "Shut up. My sister gave them to me for Christmas. She likes cows."

I crawled into bed and pulled the covers up to my waist. Carrie also hopped under the covers and we lay side by side to watch an episode of *Friends*.

When it was over, it was almost eight o'clock and Carrie said, "Maybe I should get going."

"One more episode," I said, kissing the top of her head. I had to get her to stay a little longer so I could make some moves.

"Sure." She smiled up at me.

Then we really kissed. We fumbled around under the covers for a few minutes, and soon I had her T-shirt off, and she was just in her bra.

"Aaron," she said quietly.

I didn't feel like talking but answered anyway. "Yeah?"

"I'm not ready for any more than we've already done."

She pulled away from me.

Breathing hard, I said, "Okay."

"Have you done more before?"

"Not really," I replied and stroked her hair. "Have you?"

"Can we just cuddle? I just can't do this with you yet."

I took that to mean she was a virgin just like me. I could wait. It would happen sooner or later if I played my cards right. "How about an episode of *Entourage?*"

She agreed, and we cuddled as we watched the show. Then I had to go to the bathroom.

"I'll be right back," I said.

When I returned to the bedroom, we snuggled under the covers to watch one last episode before she went home. It was only nine and she wanted to be home by ten because she had early practice. My billets were coming home around nine-thirty anyway, so that timing would work.

We both must have dozed off, because when I awoke and looked at the clock, it was past ten-thirty.

"Carrie," I said, shaking her shoulder.

She opened her eyes. "Oh no! What time is it?"

"Almost eleven!"

She jumped up. "I gotta go." She snatched her T-shirt from the bottom of the bed and quickly put it on. "I gotta pee, then I'm out of here."

Then I remembered I had forgotten to flush the toilet. My mother had drilled me about that before I left Vancouver, but because I had my own bathroom, I had kind of let that rule slip. "Sor-ry," I yelled as she was crossing the hall. "You'll have to put the seat down."

"That is so gross!" She slammed the bathroom door.

Within seconds, she was back in my room and staring at me with her mouth open and her eyes wide. "There's blood in the toilet! Like a ton of it. Are you peeing blood?"

Suddenly I heard someone coming down the stairs. My door was wide open too.

"Aaron?" It was Mrs. Dylan.

I jumped out of bed, searching for my sweatpants. Carrie picked up her books and started shoving them in her backpack.

"What are you doing?" Mrs. Dylan stood at my doorway. I was in front of her, wearing just my boxers, holding my sweatpants in my hands, totally busted.

"*What* is going on in here?" Mrs. Dylan looked at Carrie. Fortunately she was fully dressed. "Carrie, I want you to leave. Now. I need to talk to Aaron."

"But . . . Mrs. Dylan, something is wrong with Aaron. He's —"

"I said leave. Get your things and go!"

Carrie quickly gathered her things and I quickly put on my sweatpants.

When Carrie was gone, Mrs. Dylan put her hands up and said, "Aaron, I don't know what to say. I'm shocked and disappointed." She shook her head. "This matter will have to be dealt with tomorrow. I'm just too upset right now. We have young children. What were you thinking?"

"But nothing happened," I said.

"I will be talking to your coach and your parents tomorrow."

# CHAPTER EIGHTEEN

Carrie texted me when she got home. "OMG I'm so sorry."

"not your fault," I texted back.

"pee in blood whats with that?"

"dont know."

"u need to go to doc asap."

"cant think about that now."

"but could be kidneys."

"shes gonna tell coach and parents."

"crap. u gonna get kicked out."

"parents will kill me."

When we stopped texting, I went to the bathroom again. After I peed, I stared down into the toilet. The water was red. Like really red. And it had been going on since Ramsey and Killer had kicked me. I *was* peeing blood. I flushed the toilet and went back to my room. I told myself it was the least of my worries, especially now with what had just happened.

I flopped down on my bed and thought about everything. My life was a disaster. I was going to have to go back to Vancouver. I'd have no team to play on because all the teams in Vancouver were already picked.

I woke up in the middle of the night and had to go to the bathroom again. This time when I peed, it burned and the pee was crimson. I tried to convince myself it meant absolutely nothing. Was I telling myself a lie?

The next morning I got ready early and snuck out of the house. I didn't want to confront Mrs. Dylan. Maybe she wouldn't phone anyone. *Wishful thinking.*

When I was putting on my sweats for dryland, I touched my side. The pain was definitely there, and not better yet. I took two more pain-relievers before dryland. They must have worked, because I made it through without anyone suspecting anything. And Coach didn't pull me aside, so obviously Mrs. Dylan hadn't got in touch with him yet.

I went to physics but couldn't concentrate. I kept waiting for my name to be called, telling me I had to go to the office and that I was getting kicked out of my billets' house. Halfway through the class, I kept blinking to stay awake. I felt so dizzy and weak and couldn't concentrate on what the teacher was saying.

The next thing I knew, Carrie was shaking my shoulder. "What's wrong?" she asked.

I looked around. Was class over? We were the only people in the room. Had I zoned out?

She touched my forehead. "You're not hot. But something is wrong with you."

I pushed her hand away. "I'm fine." Then I got up and stumbled out of the room and into the hallway. I leaned against the wall.

Carrie had followed me. "Aaron," she said, "let me take you to the doctor."

Allie joined us. Or maybe she'd been there the whole time. "He's got the flu?" she asked. "It's going around."

"He has more than the flu," said Carrie. "He has something wrong with his kidneys. He has blood in his pee. I Googled "urine in the blood" last night and it's not good. He said he was hit in hockey. Come on. Let's go." She hooked her arm in mine.

"No," I said, refusing to go along with her. "I'll just go home and sleep it off. I'll be fine."

"I don't remember you getting hit in hockey," said Kade, eyeing me. When had he shown up? "At least not in the kidneys."

I put up my hand. "I'm going home. See you at practice."

"I'm taking you," said Carrie.

"Bad idea," I said.

"Then Allie will take you."

Allie dropped me off, and by the time I unlocked the front door, I felt absolutely awful and just wanted to sleep. I held the walls when I walked downstairs. When I hit my room, I crawled under the covers. Curled into a tight ball, I faded in and out.

The next thing I knew, Mrs. Dylan was in my room and Carrie was with her. I could hear them talking.

"I think it's his kidneys," said Carrie. "We have to get him to a medical clinic."

"No," said Mrs. Dylan. "He needs to go right to Emergency."

"Aaron." Mrs. Dylan shook my shoulder. "We need to

get you up. I have to take you to the hospital."

"I have practice," I mumbled. My thoughts went in and out and back and forth. What was happening to me?

They hoisted me up and my legs felt like mush. Carrie guided me up the stairs and into the van. I wasn't sure what was wrong. I didn't have a fever or anything but I just felt really weak and dizzy and my mouth was so dry. I couldn't think straight. We entered Emergency and the nurse took one look at me and admitted me. I told Mrs. Dylan I would be fine with the doctor by myself. Alone in the small doctor's room, I lay down on the crisp white hospital sheets.

I waited for at least twenty minutes before the doctor came in, shutting the door tightly behind him. The doctor asked me a ton of questions and I answered them all, but I still lied about how I had been hurt in the kidney, giving my story about being hit while on the ice. Then he poked my kidney, asking me where it hurt. I tried not to react to downplay it all, but in certain spots, I couldn't help wincing. After the questions, the nurse made me pee in a bottle. It wasn't long after that the doctor came back.

"You're pretty dehydrated, young man, and you're anemic from so much blood in your urine," he said. "That's what caused the dizziness. Continuing to exercise with this kind of injury didn't help you at all." He patted me on the back. "We're going to get you better and hook you up to an IV. That should help."

The nurse came back, pricked me with a needle, and attached me to a post with a bag of fluid. I closed my eyes and must have dozed. When I came to, Mrs. Dylan was by my bedside.

"Aaron," she said, stroking my forehead. "How are you feeling?"

I tried to speak but my mouth was still dry. All I could get out was a croaking sound.

She gave me a glass of water. I took a sip, then gave it back to her. "Am I going to be okay?"

"I just talked to the doctor. Your one kidney is extremely inflamed and bruised and you've lost some blood. The doctor said you must have suffered a really bad blow. You lost a lot of fluids and blood, which didn't help. That's why you felt so sick. They might run a few more tests on your urinary system just to make sure everything is okay."

"Where's Carrie?"

"She was here for over an hour. I told her to go to her practice."

"Did I miss my practice?"

"I'm afraid so."

"Did you talk to my coach?"

"Yes." She paused. "But only about you being sick. I will deal with the other stuff separately. I also called your parents. I told them you were going to be fine but they insisted on flying out tonight."

I could feel tears behind my eyes. I didn't want to cry in front of Mrs. Dylan, but everything just seemed so wrong. "I don't want them to take me home." I rolled my head to look at her. "And I don't want you to kick me out of your house. I'm so sorry, Mrs. Dylan. Nothing happened. And it won't ever happen."

She touched my face as a mother would. "I'm not going to kick you out. But we will talk later to set up some house rules. Right now, you have to get well."

"How long do I have to stay in the hospital?"

"Thanks to Carrie, you won't have to stay in here long. Thankfully, she called me from school. Like I said, they want to run a few more tests. I think they will take you to a room and make you stay overnight. But you could be out as early as tomorrow morning."

"Will I get to play this weekend?"

"I don't think so. Do you remember being hit?"

I turned my head so she couldn't see my face. Somehow I had to deal with this, and there was only one way to do it.

# CHAPTER NINETEEN

Kade came to the hospital that evening. "Hey," he said.

I had fallen asleep again and he woke me up. "How was practice?" I muttered.

"Good." He drummed his fingers on his thighs. Over and over.

"Listen," he finally said. "I heard Rammer talking to Killer. They didn't see me follow them down the hall. What did they do to you?"

"It doesn't matter."

"Wonger, they did something. I could tell they were scared. And they kept saying no one could find out. It's not right. You have to say something."

I looked at the ceiling.

"Then I'll say something." Kade yanked his phone out of his jacket pocket. "I'm phoning Rennert. And I'm telling him about the rookie party too. Those guys can't do shit like this and get away with it."

"Kade, don't." I paused for a second. "I'm going to tell him."

"You're sure?"

"Yeah. I'm sure."

Kade had just left when Carrie walked in, carrying a colourful gift bag. My call would have to wait a few more minutes.

"I brought you something." She smiled.

I sat up, the pain excruciating, and opened the bag. It contained a *Hockey Now* magazine and a little teddy bear. Normally stuffed animals weren't my thing, but because it came from Carrie, I liked it. A lot. "Thanks," I said. "You didn't have to get me anything you know. I'm only in here for one night and that's just because they want to run a bunch of stupid tests."

"I know it's moronic to give you a stuffed animal, but I couldn't help it. He was so cute."

I laughed, then groaned at the sharp pain.

She took my hand in hers. "Aaron, what happened? You have to come clean. When I helped Mrs. Dylan take you to the hospital, you were, like, out of it, and you mumbled something about Rammer and Killer."

I closed my eyes. There were moments in the past ten hours I couldn't remember.

She squeezed my hand. "Rammer has issues for sure, but that doesn't mean he can get away with everything."

"Issues? You mean because of his dad?"

"Yeah." She sighed and sat down on the edge of the bed. "When we hooked up that night, we talked about a lot of things. I could relate to him because we both had so much crap going on. That's why I thought I could trust him and why what he did was so hurtful. But it's also a big part of why I didn't say anything. His father was verbally and physically abusive to him when he was young. If he didn't score a bunch of goals, he got really mad at him and stuff like that. He nicknamed him Loser."

"I called him a loser," I said. "It must have set him off."

"He needs help. That's why you have to say something."

I nodded. "Did Mrs. Dylan say anything to you about last night?" I asked.

"Yeah, we talked." She stared at the bedsheet she was twisting around her finger. "We had time in the waiting room." She looked at me. "I don't think she's going to rat us out, but, Aaron, we have to be more careful. We've been playing with the rules. It's wrong. I like the school and I want to go on in synchro, perform in Vegas or something. And I know you want to get a scholarship. There's no point ruining it for ourselves."

I exhaled. "My parents are coming sometime tonight."

"Are they going to freak?"

"Freak? It's my mother's middle name. She hates hockey and now this. She'll want me to come home."

"Will you?"

"Will I what?"

"Go home?"

"I hope not."

"Can I meet them?"

I grinned. "Now who's the one moving too fast?"

She playfully slapped my arm. "Shut up."

"Okay, but won't you find meeting my parents awkward?"

"You can meet *my* mom," she replied. "She's easy. But never my dad." She paused. "Hey, you hungry?" she asked, changing the subject. "I can go get you some real food."

Five minutes later Carrie left to get me a hamburger and french fries. And she also left me her cell phone because mine was back at the house in my backpack. I figured it was as good a time as any to call Coach Rennert.

He answered after the first ring.

"Coach," I said, my throat instantly drying up.

"Aaron. I'm coming to visit after I finish my paperwork. How are you?"

"Um, I need . . ." I cleared my throat. "I need to talk to you about . . . some things."

"Okay. Go ahead."

"No. Not by phone," I said.


An hour later Coach Rennert walked into my room. Carrie had left not long before. He pulled a chair close to my bed and sat. "How are you feeling?"

"Okay. I'll be back on the ice by the end of the week." Maybe if I said this aloud, I could make myself believe it.

"No need to rush things." Then he got right to the point. "What happened, Aaron? What do you need to tell me?"

He stayed silent, waiting for me to speak. This was it. I had to talk. "Ramsey and Kilby cornered me." I paused. I swallowed. Then I took a deep breath, which shot a pain right through my body.

"I want the entire story," said Coach Rennert.

"Okay. Ramsey told me you wanted to see me. When I went down the hallway to the back office, they were there and they pushed me outside." I looked away. I still didn't want to be a rat. But I had to tell him. "They, uh, kicked and punched me. I think the kick was what hurt my kidney."

He pressed his lips together so hard they turned white. I thought he was going to blow. But then his shoulders sagged, and he closed his eyes. He blew out some air and his tough demeanour disappeared. He ran his hand through his hair. "I apologize, Aaron. I put him in charge of the team."

"There's more," I said, turning my face away.

"Go on."

"The rookie party didn't go so well."

He didn't say anything for a moment. I looked at him. "Because?"

I knew he wanted me to finish what I started, but now that I had, I just couldn't. "Don't make me talk about it, okay? I can't. And what they wanted to happen ... well ... I got away before ..."

He sucked in a big breath through his nostrils. Then he put a hand on my arm and looked directly into my eyes. "Aaron, what did they do?"

I swallowed. Then said, "They tried to shove a bottle up me." I fought tears. "I'm sorry, Coach."

"You have nothing to be sorry about. It shouldn't have come to this point. I trusted my leadership. I guess I got conned too." He stood and patted me on the shoulder. "Get better. We're going to need you in the lineup."

My parents arrived after visiting hours. I totally expected my mom to start shrieking in Chinese, but instead she smoothed my hair off my forehead and said, "Aaron, this is no good." Then she pulled up my covers, tucking me in.

"I'm okay," I said. Her touch did make me feel better. And a lump suddenly formed in my throat, although I fought it. "I think I'm getting out in the morning."

"I talked to you last night," said my father. "Why didn't you tell me you were sick?"

"Well, I wasn't really sick then. Besides, you were worried about my English grade."

"I don't know about this school, Aaron." My dad sighed and ran his hand through his hair. "What boys do this kind of thing?"

*What? How did they know anything?* "Who talked to you?"

"We met with your coach," said my dad. "He bought us coffee."

"He said some boys tried to hurt you," my mom said. She grabbed a tissue and wiped her eyes. "All they do is fight in hockey. It's not good."

I pressed my head against the pillow. My mother always thought the worst and that was partly because Vancouver was overrun with gangs, especially in the East Side where most of the Chinese-Canadians lived. Hopefully, they didn't know about the rookie party.

But then my dad said, "The school doesn't put up with any sort of . . . hazing or bullying. I don't know what this hazing is." He paused before he added, "We told you not to go to parties."

I wondered how much they knew. I had a feeling Coach Rennert hadn't filled them in completely. So I ignored the party part and said, "Listen, the school is really good. And you just said they won't put up with bullying." I waited a beat, then said, "I don't want to leave. I want to stay. I've started playing pretty good. I'm learning a lot."

"We know," said my father. "Your coach thinks you have great potential and you could get a scholarship."

"Then there's no need for me to come home, Dad," I said. "The rest of the guys are great. And the hockey is good. And if you fight, you get suspended."

"Maybe we should press assault charges against those boys," said my dad.

"No, don't," I replied.

"What they did is against the law." My father crossed his arms.

"Dad, don't make this worse than it already is."

"We'll see, Aaron. This is not your decision."

# CHAPTER TWENTY

I was released from the hospital the next morning, but the doctors said I needed to take a few days off school and hockey, to allow my kidney to heal. Being in bed was not my choice, that's for sure. Especially when I knew that, by now, the school was involved and decisions were being made about the hockey team.

There was a rumour the entire team could get suspended for the year. We were not allowed on the ice until the situation was dealt with. It made me sick to my stomach to think I was involved in all this. I knew Ramsey and Kilby had been suspended indefinitely, but the final decision about the team and them was still in some sort of negotiation.

Kade phoned me constantly to tell me what was going on. He said there was another rumour that Ramsey's dad had totally flipped out when he heard Tony was suspended, and he'd stormed into Coach Rennert's office, trying to get him to fight. Security was called and he was hauled out of the arena. People were also saying that he had done the same thing with Ramsey, his own son, only this time he got the punches in.

I honestly felt bad for Ramsey. My parents might not support everything I do, but my dad would never hit me.

I watched every *Planet Earth* video I had, and *Entourage* over and over again. And I did a little homework. I wrote an English essay that was due soon. My parents got a hotel room, so they could stay in Calgary for a few days and monitor my progress. My sister was staying at a friend's and that suited her just fine.

After two whole days of nothing, I was allowed to go to school. A meeting had been set up in the principal's office for ten o'clock my first day back.

"Thank God you're here," said Allie when I walked into physics class. "I need help."

"Yeah, physics hasn't been the same," said Carrie, smiling. I hadn't seen her since the hospital — we'd thought it best if she didn't visit me while I was in bed, although we did talk and text a lot.

"It was so boring at the house," I replied. "I'm actually glad to be back at school."

The teacher started talking and I focused my attention on what he was saying. After all, I had missed a few days. Halfway through class, at five to ten, I gathered up my books, my heart racing. Time to go to the principal's office.

Carrie saw me preparing to leave and whispered, "Good luck."

"Thanks," I said.

My parents met me outside the principal's office and we entered together. Immediately I saw that I was joining a meeting with Tony Ramsey and his mother — no father — Steven Kilby, and both his parents, plus Coach Rennert.

Sweat beaded on my forehead. I hadn't been in contact with the guys since I'd landed in the hospital and heard rumblings that they might get kicked out of the school forever. Ramsey glanced at me briefly before he hung his head again. And Killer looked at me for all of a second, but that was it. Then he looked away.

"Have a seat, Mr. and Mrs. Wong, Aaron," said Mr. Marks, the principal.

I sat. This was the most awkward moment of my life.

"We have some things to discuss," the principal began. "Coach Rennert specifically asked that the three boys and their parents be here together. We wanted to wait until Aaron was well enough to attend school."

He turned to my parents. "Are you going to press charges, Mr. and Mrs. Wong?"

Before my parents could answer, I blurted out, "No, Dad. Don't do that."

The room took on an eerie silence for a few seconds. Then Tony Ramsey said, "Mr. and Mrs. Wong, I'm really sorry for what I did to your son." He stopped, took a breath, and turned to me. "Aaron, I'm so sorry. It was wrong. It shouldn't have happened."

For the first time since I entered the room, I really looked at Ramsey. His smirk was gone, and all I could see on his face was remorse and a purple bruise under one eye. I honestly felt for him. His dad was obviously a real bastard.

Steven tried to speak, but Ramsey interrupted him. "Dude," he said, "it was my fault, not yours." Then he looked at Coach Rennert. "Coach, I don't think anyone else should be punished but me." His voice quivered. "I was the acting captain and I coerced Steven into helping me. He lowered his head and I saw his shoulders start to shake. "I . . . I told him he'd get kicked off the team if he told or didn't . . . listen to me."

"I'm to blame too," said Steven quietly. "Aaron, I'm sorry too. Like, really sorry." He hung his head. "I've never done anything like this before. And I'll never do it again."

I saw Steven's mother put her hand on his, and his father rest his hand on Steven's shoulder.

"As a family," said Mr. Kilby, "we will accept any consequences you think are appropriate for Steven. What he did was wrong and he knows that."

Mr. Marks looked at my parents. "Mr. and Mrs. Wong, it's your choice. You can press charges if you'd like."

I knew enough to stay quiet and that my parents really did have the final decision. I'd said what I could. After a few seconds, my father said, "Perhaps there should be other consequences for these boys."

"I agree," said Coach Rennert, the first he'd spoken at the meeting. I looked over at him and immediately saw the strained lines on his face. He, like the rest of us, didn't want our team suspended for the year. All of us would be going home if that happened.

The principal looked sternly at Tony and Steven. "You boys are lucky. What you did is against the law." Then he looked at the parents. "I'm afraid the school has strict policies against this kind of behaviour, and we can't let your boys off easy."

# CHAPTER TWENTY-ONE

I sat in the stands, dressed in a suit and tie. Coach Rennert had given me the job of taking stats, because the doctor had said I couldn't play the weekend games. Coach had also had a big talk with the team about what had happened at the rookie party. Everyone was relieved that the school didn't suspend the entire team. Tony and Steven had been kicked out of the school, sent home, and had no team to play on for the entire year. The Podium Hockey Team had been put on probation, and if we did one more stupid thing, there would be no hockey team for us either for the rest of the year and Coach Rennert would lose his job. We could all kiss Podium and hockey goodbye for the season.

My parents had flown home because, well, they weren't going to watch a hockey game if they didn't know any of the players. Everything was getting back to normal with them and I wasn't getting my sticks until Christmas. I had to get my English mark up first.

I figured I could remedy that one and perhaps they would miss me again once they got home. I did want to see my sister before Christmas, so I planned to work on my parents and get them to come to Kelowna when we played there in November.

Carrie knew enough not to sit with me at a game when I had a job to do. I liked that about her; she understood sport. That was one reason my previous girlfriend only lasted two weeks; she was always jealous of my hockey. Not Carrie.

Coach had shuffled the lines around, and with three players missing, they were working with just three lines. I would be back for the next game and a rumour circulated that the coaches were trying to recruit more players to fill the two empty spots. Kade was worried. He had moved up to the second line and wanted to stay there.

As I watched, I studied the players and how they were positioning themselves on the ice. Hockey was like a chess game with players moving all the time, trying to find the best spot to be. Max was good — he read the ice. Kade always finished his checks. Kurt moved the puck well. Those were all things I needed to do better. By the end of the game, I had at least ten things I needed to work on when I got back on the ice next week.

After the game, which ended in a 4–4 tie, I took the stats sheets to Coach Rennert. He was back to his one-word answers and stiff-as-a-board approach. Since the incident, he had been super strict. One step out of line and a player would be turfed from the team. He took the stats, said thanks, and walked away. I went into the dressing room.

Hot Dog was hanging up his jersey with the C on it. Coach Rennert had announced before the game that for a while, the *C* would rotate. He wanted to be extremely selective about his choice of Captain. Ben and I, as rookies, were going to share the other *A*. I would wear it for all the away games and he would wear it for all the home games. The guys had actually cheered when they heard that news.

I sat beside Kade. "Good game."

"Thanks." He tossed his shoulder pads in his bag. "We still going to eat?"

"Allie and Carrie said they'd meet us there in an hour."

"Sounds good. I'm starving."

"Yeah, me too." All week I had been forced to talk to my coaches, teachers, parents, billets, and now it was Friday and I just wanted to have a normal night. I was talked out and sick of the word *hazing*. I wanted to have some fun — with no alcohol, of course.

"Wonger," said Max, "catch." He threw his tape at me. I caught it and threw it back.

He grinned at me. "You're okay, Wonger." He knew he was lucky to still be at Podium.

Next thing I knew, tape was flying all around the room. Even though I was dressed in a suit, I jumped up and joined the battle, laughing with every toss and duck.

# ACKNOWLEDGEMENTS

My first huge thank you goes to Carrie Gleason and Jim Lorimer for having enough faith in me, and my writing, to start a brand new sports series. I am so grateful for their time, effort and commitment in developing the Podium Sports Academy Series. I had the idea for this series for many years and Lorimer was the only publisher I approached with it because I knew they would do the series justice. A big thanks goes to all the Sports Schools and Academies around the world, because they do encourage teens to reach their athletic potential. I put many schools together to create Podium. And, a big thank you goes to the Lorimer design team. Behind the scenes they work diligently to create logos, covers and make the content look awesome. It really did take a team to put this series together. And, to my wonderful reader, thank you for reading the words I write.

*Rookie* is Lorna Schultz Nicholson's ninth novel and the first book in her Podium Sports Academy series. Lorna is also the author of seven non-fiction books about hockey. Growing up in St. Catharines, Ontario, Lorna played volleyball, basketball, soccer, softball, and hockey and was also a member of the Canadian National Rowing Team. She attended the University of Victoria, British Columbia, where she obtained a Bachelor of Science degree in Human Performance. From there Lorna worked in recreation centres, health clubs, and as a rowing coach until she turned her attention to writing. Today Lorna works as a full-time writer and does numerous school and library visits throughout the year to talk about her books. She divides her time between Calgary, Alberta, and Penticton, British Columbia, and lives with her husband, Hockey Canada President Bob Nicholson, her son who plays junior hockey, and various hockey players who billet at their home for several months of the year. She also has two daughters who now live away from home, but thankfully, the two dogs and the cat are still around to keep her company while she writes.

*"Lorna's books are a great read for kids and their parents. They really help teach the importance of having good values both in hockey and in life."*

— Wayne Gretzky

## DON'T MISS THIS BOOK!

# VEGAS TRYOUT

" It's Vegas. And Vegas is all about how you look.

"You need to lose at least ten pounds." Coach snapped her book shut. "This had better change by next weigh-in. You're the shortest girl on this team and now you're the heaviest."

Lap after lap, I swam as hard as I could to get my frustration out.

Suck it up and swim, Carrie. "

Synchro swimmer Carrie doesn't have the body shape that most athletes in her sport have, so when her coach takes her off the lift and puts her on a special diet, Carrie takes it too far.

Available Spring 2012

Buy the books online at www.lorimer.ca